Dedication

For Amelia, Billy, Josh, and Maddy
&
For everyone connected with the wonderful
Derian House Children's Hospice, Chorley.

Acknowledgements

The source documents, internet sites, and contacts for my research, were too numerous to include in their entirety. The few mentioned below are ones that readers may find particularly interesting if they wish to dig deeper behind the some of the personal stories told by the young people in this book.

CSCA - *The Proficient Caver's Information Book.* English Nature – *The Ingleborough Ridge Route.* The Somali Muslim Community in England. *Shabelle News.* The Home Office media centre regarding male forced marriage. The Foreign and Commonwealth Office Forced Marriage Unit. *"Young Women With Anorexsia Nervosa Speak Out About Hospital Experiences"* – A Dissertation by Jaqueline Segal. 2003. *"Winton's Children."* http://www.just-powell.co.uk/winton/ The MailOnline Thursday, Aug 18 2011 *"British Schindler welcomes steam train carrying evacuees he helped to escape the Holocaust as children."*

And for those who wish to know more about the way in which anti-gang strategies operate in the UK and the USA - *My Fellowship July-August 2010 by Donna Marsh, On Gangs.* –Winston Churchill Memorial Trust. The Jewish joke repeated by Asif is well known in that community and appears in many forms, but its origin is unknown.

And last, but not least, my thanks to the Bolton Writers Group for their comments on *The Cave* and help in proofing *A Trace of Blood.*

THE CAVE

by

Bill Rogers

C A T O N

Published in 2011 by Caton Books

First Edition

Published by Caton Books 2011

www.catonbooks.com

ISBN: 978-0-9564220-5-7

Cover Design by Dragonfruit
Design & Layout by Commercial Campaigns

Chapter 1

It happened nearly two years ago. May 30th to be precise. I needed to put some distance between myself and those events, but I also had to write it down while it was still reasonably fresh in my mind. Not that I'm likely to forget. There's no chance of that. What happened changed my life. I'm not sure how, I just know that it has.

We were headlines for the first two days. The television, newspapers, and radio were over us like a rash. But they didn't tell the real story. All they were interested in was who the heroes were, who to blame, what it felt like, and who suffered most; us or our loved ones.

Don't get me wrong, they didn't tell any lies, or make anything up, they were just not interested in the really important questions. Like, what did we learn about ourselves, about each other, about life...about death? That's why I'm telling my story, my version of what happened. And because I owe it to the ones who did not survive.

I contacted the others and asked did they mind. I had to because we had this confidentiality agreement. To my surprise, nobody did. Jag said it was a waste of time because he'd already spilt the beans on Facebook. What he actually said was:

'Grace, is dat a re-question? Cos you an' me know you already dee-cided. It's piff by me co-dee, but you clappin, cos I already told dat on de big FB!'

So it looks like Jag hasn't changed after all, or maybe he just doesn't know it yet.

It was the Spring of 2009. There were thirty of us, all from the West Manchester Leadership Academy. I know it sounds pretentious, like they can spot a future leader at eleven and a half years of age, or guarantee to turn you into one by the time you leave seven years later, which for me will be in a few months time

You are probably wondering what a Leadership Academy is? Good question. Here's a better one. What kind of person do they want you to become? The reason it's a better question is that the answer is carved in foot high letters across the red sandstone portico at the entrance to the school.

STRIVE SCHOOL

It's a mnemonic, and the words that it represents are repeated in glossy posters all over the school, in every assembly, whenever we achieve something special, and whenever we transgress. They are supposed to sum up what we need in order to become better persons and better leaders:

Strivers to Achieve; Responsible; Inspiring; Visionary; Emotionally-intelligent; Self-motivating; Courageous; Honest; Open-minded; Optimistic; Lifelong Learners.

After the first few weeks nobody bothered to look up at the ceiling anymore. Whatever, those words hung over us like the sword of Damocles.

Every year we had to go on an outdoors education trip for a week, staying in a youth hostel, or a camp.

That year there were five different venues for Year 10 and 11 students. The one that I was selected for was situated between the Southern Lakes and the Central Pennine range. For the first time we were in mixed class groups. I've since discovered that there were two reasons for this. They wanted to take us out of our comfort zones, and they wanted to pair up some of the most confident among us, with some of the least confident. The idea was to test and develop our emotional intelligence, and in particular our mentoring skills.

We were tested way beyond anything they, or we, could have imagined.

We arrived on the Saturday morning, and set up camp in a wood pungent with the smell of wild garlic. Then we each had to construct a bivouac. Mine was a complete disaster because I could not get the branches to bend properly. Every time I came close they sprung back without warning. I have a small crescent shaped scar on my left shoulder to prove it. I cannot believe that it's the only physical reminder I have of that week spent in the Pennines. In the afternoon we abseiled off the rocks near Ingleton while other groups went canoeing or fell walking.

'Don't spend all night sitting up chatting,' Miss Walsh advised us. 'The next few days you're really going to need to keep your wits about you.'

Poor Miss Walsh, she really had not the faintest idea how those words would come back to haunt us.

Chapter 2
Sunday May 29th

Another scorching day, baking the stones that lined the river bank, blinding us with reflections from water the colour of jade.

They drove us north in the minibuses and, after the regulation half an hour's instruction, let us loose on the *Go Ape* trail in Grizedale Forest. That was when we first bonded as a group. There were eight of us, each from a different tutor group, hanging about in the trees; literally hanging, from harnesses and zip wires, high in the forest canopy. I can see us now, as clear as day.

Daniel, tall and lean, with a serious expression on a face surrounded by a mass of dark brown curls, waited patiently for the person ahead of him to edge through a tunnel linking his tree with the next. Beside him, blonde haired, blue eyed Naomi, the only American among us, tightened the harness another notch around her ominously thin frame. Daniel turned, looked down at Naomi, and said something reassuring. Head lowered, she whispered her reply forcing him to lean closer, his arm around her shoulder. She shrank at his touch, twisting away her pale face with its pinched cheeks and downturned mouth.

Twenty metres ahead, in stark contrast, statuesque Amina stood, hands on hips, as she watched her companion climb the final rungs of the ladder bolted to the trunk above her. A ray of sunlight slanting through a gap between the pines caught her face in profile, burnishing cheeks the colour of coffee. Amina smiled as Devon stepped out onto the walkway, leant back against the trunk, and glanced tentatively down hoping for her approval. Her smile broadened as she raised her thumb and nodded her head. It was a simple gesture, but one that lit up his face in a way that I had never seen before. Quiet and unobtrusive, ordinary to the point of near invisibility, Devon had ghosted his way through three and half years at West Manchester Academy. His attention was distracted by a cry from up ahead.

Wesley, built like an athlete, launched himself into the abyss. He soared through the air on a Tarzan swing hurtling towards a web of woven ropes. At the last moment he plummeted confidently into the rigging, releasing the adrenalin rush with a final triumphant yell. Behind him, awaiting his turn, squat, square jawed, Jag punched the air and shouted in admiration of his hero.

'Totally insane in'it?!'

Beside me Charlie withdrew a little more into himself. Bad enough that he had to clip himself onto the zip wire, step off the platform, and fly like a bullet through the trees into the unknown; even worse that Wesley and Jag and I would be sensing his fear, contemptuous of his timidity, impatient for our turn.

'It'll be fine Charlie,' I said. 'The instructor's waiting at the other end, and you've seen how soft the landing is.'

In truth, I was a little scared myself. I knew they wouldn't risk any harm coming to us but there is a big difference between knowing and doing. This must be how those celebrities feel in the jungle. And right now the only way we were going to get out of there was to step off that platform.

Charlie's hand was shaking. He was never going to manage that clip unaided. But I didn't want to patronise him; especially with the others watching.

'One step at a time Charlie,' I told him calmly. 'Hold onto the wire with your left hand. That's it. Now press down on the clip on your karabiner with your thumb, and keep it pressed down. Well done.'

His hand continued to shake but the clip was open. 'OK,' I said. 'Now raise your right hand, get it into position on the pulley, and gently remove your thumb. Well done.'

I could tell that there was no way he would take that final step. We could hear Wesley encouraging Jag to follow him on the Tarzan swing. It was ironic, yet perfectly in character, that Jag who worked so hard at portraying a big tough macho image was turning out to be only marginally less insecure than Charlie.

They had impressed on us during the training that on no account should we force anyone to climb, or crawl, or jump or swing, or doing anything they didn't want to do. That it was all about encouragement and support. So far that had worked, although everyone had been muttering about how long it had taken me to persuade Charlie to tackle every obstacle on the course. We should have gone last, not first, but it was too late to do anything about that now.

Here we were, the two of us, facing Charlie's Waterloo. I knew that this time, whatever I said, he was not going to hear me. His brain had closed down. The previous term, in biology, Mrs Jaroslaw had taught us about the reptilian brain, and how in moments of fear or challenge it goes into one mode or the other, fight or flight. Well Charlie had fled. And he was not coming back. His body was rigid, as though frozen. I couldn't hear him breathing and I wasn't even sure if he had a pulse.

There was a yell behind us. Jag was clambering triumphantly up the side of the netting. Any moment now they would be heading our way. I couldn't let them see Charlie like this. I took a deep breath, bent down as though checking my boot laces, and appeared to lose my balance, cannoning into Charlie before dangling suspended from my own harness on the safety wire.

I watched as Charlie disappeared soundlessly between the trees, skimming the bushes as he headed for journey's end.

Wesley climbed up onto the platform.

'I didn't know he had in him,' he said hauling me onto my feet. 'Are you alright Grace? Not like you to lose your footing.'

'He's tougher than you think,' I replied, attaching my Karabiner to the zip wire pulley. I was anxious to check that Charlie was alright. Without a moment's hesitation, I launched myself.

The air whistled like a gentle wind through my hair, cooling my face. The only sound was the buzz of the pulley on the wire. I felt an indescribable sense of peace, of freedom. I could stay up here forever.

I emerged from the trees into bright sunlight, high above a valley lush with grass and dotted with purple orchids. The angle of the wire steepened. With a sudden burst of speed I hurtled towards the landing stage. Legs out in front I braced myself for contact. One heel touched and my body spun sickeningly through 180 degrees. Landing backside first I scooped up woodchips like a shovel, filling my knickers and jeans to the tops of my boots.

Charlie stood behind the wooden rails clapping his hands and grinning all over his face. That's what I meant about bonding.

What none of us knew was how much and how cruelly those bonds would be tested in the days ahead.

Chapter 3
Monday May 30th

If anything, Monday was even hotter. They decided to take us underground. The least experienced groups left first for a guided tour of the White Scar show caves. The rest of us – our team of eight and another of nine – were promised a special treat.

'A real adventure and a proper challenge,' said Matt the lead instructor. Having had plenty of practice on the climbing wall at school, proved our ability to abseil, and done a little caving the previous year in the Cheddar Gorge, we were to explore a part of the cave system not open to tourists or casual visitors.

At eleven o'clock in the morning we gathered excitedly in the entrance to the cave complex.

'Beneath your feet,' Matt explained once we'd quietened down. 'There is a hidden world spanning three counties, Lancashire, Yorkshire, and Cumbria, a world of subterranean streams, of lakes, of halls, and galleries where few have trod. At this moment, less than a half a mile from here, a team of cavers – the Misty Mountain Mud Miners - are about to fulfil a lifelong dream. To break through a wall of mud and rock and link these tunnels into the longest continuous accessible system of caves in Britain, and one of the longest on this planet. The minute you step inside this cave you will become a part of history.'

We were in awe, not least the girls. Matt was every young woman's dream, and every young man's hero. Approaching six foot tall, with broad shoulders and a lithe yet muscular frame apparent even through his bright yellow caving suit, he was a commanding presence. He had the knack of making you feel as though he was speaking only to you. I could tell that even Miss Walsh, standing on a raised stone beside me, was spellbound, and she was supposed to be getting married in the summer holidays.

'When my colleagues have achieved their goal people will flock from all over the world to explore these caves.' Matt looked at each of us in turn, the silence pregnant with anticipation. 'You will have been here first.'

The applause was instantaneous; bouncing off the walls and roof of the walk-in entrance where we stood, echoing down the tunnels stretching out ahead of us. It is a sound that haunts me still.

Matt led us off in single file. Our spirits were high and you could feel the excitement. Even though we had been told that it would be challenging he had assured as it would not be dangerous. No more so than taking a moonlit walk in the woods. Providing that we did exactly as we were told. Even Charlie seemed relaxed.

The beams from our headlamps cast weird shadows darting back and forth at random. At first the passage was wide and high, the walls, ceiling and floor a uniform limestone grey, streaked here and there with bands of reddish brown. The well trod path of the dried up river bed was smooth and easy under foot.

The passage narrowed abruptly into a tunnel where we were forced to crawl for several minutes on hands and knees up a steady incline. I sensed that behind me Charlie was finding it hard going, and slowed my own pace so that I didn't lose touch with him.

A half an hour later we emerged into a vast cavern over forty metres in diameter, and almost as much in height, from which radiated six more tunnels of varying breadth. Bright white needles the thickness of a finger, and over a metre long, hung suspended from the ceiling like a giant's pin cushion. Towards the furthest wall, beckoning us to join him, stood Matt with his back to a sudden drop into which gushed a metre wide waterfall. The sound reverberated around the walls.

'Come closer,' he shouted above the roar. 'But stay well away from the edge.'

Charlie squeezed himself into the gap between Devon and me, staring apprehensively over his shoulder into the black hole into which the cascade disappeared.

'This is the Devil's Hole,' Matt proclaimed theatrically. 'No explanation required I'm sure you'll agree.' He pointed towards the ceiling. 'And these are what exactly?'

Our hands went up, but Jag didn't wait to be asked. 'Stalagmites,' he said.

A universal groan went up and someone muttered 'Pillock.'

'Stalactites,' Jag blustered. 'I meant stalactites.' His embarrassment was painfully apparent in the harsh glare of our headlamps.

'Which is it?' Matt asked.

'Stalac*tites*!' we chorused.

'How do you know?'

'Ants in the pants,' said Daniel. 'The mites go up, and the tights come down.'

'I didn't know you wore tights Daniel,' said Miss Walsh.

That had us all laughing, including Daniel.

'Very good,' said Matt. 'And what do we call a hole like this one behind me?'

'A sink hole,' ventured Amina.

'Or a swallow hole?' I suggested.

'You're both right,' said Matt. 'And how was it formed?'

'By the acid in groundwater and rainwater seeping through cracks and faults in the rock and dissolving the limestone over time,' Wesley said confidently.

It was a textbook answer. We all turned to look at him. Wesley was tall for his age, good looking, and broad shouldered. He was also the centre half and captain of the Senior football team; definitely fanciable, but well out of my league. Still, it didn't stop a girl dreaming.

'Spot on,' said Matt. 'This began as a solutional cave above the water table, that over time has seen groundwater recharge create a number of tributary streams. Those streams produced these passages you can see branching off in different directions. So it is also a branchwork cave.'

Interesting as it was I hoped he wasn't going to go on much longer. It was cold and damp this close to the freezing waterfall, and I was beginning to lose the feeling in my fingers. Beside me Charlie was shivering. Heaven knows how Naomi must have felt without an ounce of fat on her.

'We're going to start off down that passage over there,' he said, pointing to his right. 'You'll be able to stand for the first twenty metres or so, then I'm afraid it's hands and knees up a thirty metre pitch. The tunnel narrows as it meets another passage at right angles; a sort of T junction. You'll have to squeeze through a hole we call the letterbox. You'll see why when you come to it. This next passage we'll have to navigate lying down, using arms and legs the way I'm told you've practised before. It shouldn't be a problem for any of you. If you find it a squeeze, release your backpack and push it ahead of you. And believe me, it'll be worth it when you see what's on the other side. I'll lead, and Ms Walsh will bring up the rear? Any questions?'

Thankfully there were none. We set off in single file. Daniel was immediately behind Matt, then came Amina, Naomi, Jag, Devon, me, then Charlie, Wesley and Ms Walsh. Nobody chose that order, it just happened. I suppose that's what's meant by fate.

The going was easy at first. Even on the crawl section the floor was smooth and dry, and the height and width of the passage though snug was far from claustrophobic.

The tunnel levelled off towards the end and changed in composition. There were rocks that ranged from the size of tennis balls to small boulders that came together in a wall across the width of the tunnel. In the centre, half a metre from the floor, a roughly rectangular opening had been created just large enough to accommodate an average adult human being. Devon's lower legs and boots protruded as he hauled himself further into the cavity.

'I don't like it Grace,' whispered Charlie, peering around my shoulder, the beam from his headlamp flickering nervously on the sloping roof.

'You'll be fine Charlie,' I reassured him. 'Devon's twice your size and look how easy it is for him.'

I could tell he wasn't convinced, and that nothing I could say would make any difference; best to keep moving, and hope that he'd follow.

'As soon as my boots are clear follow me Charlie,' I said firmly. 'I'll take it steady, so you'll always be able to see them. You can even hang on to them if you need to.'

Without waiting for a reply I pushed my head and shoulders over the rim, and used my elbows to push myself into the void. I could see Devon up ahead. Somehow he had managed to turn onto his back and was using his feet to push against the floor enabling him to wriggle like a worm, head first up the gentle incline, the beam from his headlamp sweeping across the roof. I decide not to follow suit. I was worried that my back pack would be damaged, and in any case I wanted to see where I was going. I didn't have Devon's blind faith in our leader, gorgeous though he was, or in my helmet.

Once I'd progressed a full body length I stopped and listened hard. There was the scraping sound of boots and clothing scuffing the limestone surface, and muffled voices ahead and behind me.

'Charlie, are you there?' I called.

For a long moment I thought I'd made a mistake to leave him there. Then I felt a tentative tug on my left boot, and knew that he was with me.

'Well done Charlie,' I told him. 'Keep coming, we'll be there in no time.'

It was further than I'd anticipated. According to my watch we had been inching forward for almost five minutes. I know it doesn't sound long but imagine being stuck in a lift that long with nothing but a torch for company. If I was beginning to feel hemmed in what must Charlie have been feeling. The only clue was the way his little hand had steadily tightened around my ankle to the point where he was now like a dead weight I had to drag along behind me.

The end came without warning. The passageway narrowed, curved to the left, straightened out and dipped abruptly. I felt Charlie's fingers lose their grip on my ankle as I slid down a slope as smooth as marble onto the floor of another cave. I sat up and turned just as Charlie popped out like a cork from a bottle, cannoning into me and throwing us both to the ground. I could feel him shaking with laughter and relief.

'Come on,' I said, pushing him off and rolling clear. 'We don't want Wesley landing on top of us.'

We brushed ourselves down and started to walk over towards the others who were grouped around Matt. Halfway there I stopped and stared in amazement.

Half the size of the previous chamber what this one lacked in dimension it more than made up for in appearance. Oval in shape, with a flat floor bed and a gently curving roof, the surfaces were uniformly smooth except at what my compass later informed me was the northern end.

There was a pool ten metres in diameter. On the left a pale pink mass of limestone, suspended from the roof by a single column, draped like a shroud to the water's edge. At the furthest rim the wall became a bank rising four metres to a shelf that opened out into another smaller cave partially in shadow. Four sturdy stalagmites, the size of pavement bollards, sprouted randomly from the top of the shelf. On the roof above, a cluster of shorter thinner stalactites hung needle like. In the eerie golden glow of our lamps the overall effect was of a pair of giant, open mouthed, gap toothed toads reflected perfectly in a shimmering pool.

'Who was behind you Charlie?' asked Matt.

'I don't know,' he replied, looking to me for an answer.

'Come on Charlie,' I said. 'Who was it we didn't want to land on top of us?'

A smile lit his face. 'Wesley,' he said.

'Well he should be out by now,' said Matt striding over towards the passage from which we had come. He stuck his head inside, listened for a moment, called out, and listened again. He stood up and slipped his pack from his back. 'It looks as though Wesley is stuck where the passage narrows. He probably twisted a little too far. It happens. I'll just go and help him to free himself.In the meantime nobody wanders off exploring. You stay together right where you are. Understood?'

We watched him enter that black hole, and begin to haul himself up the slippery slope until he had disappeared.

Less than a minute of mindless chatter had passed when the ground seemed to move beneath my feet. I knew the others felt it too because Charlie grabbed my arm, and nobody spoke. Ten seconds later a stronger tremor caused us all to hang on to each other. Jag started to swear, and a scream seemed to catch in Naomi's throat; emerging like the strangled sound that foxes make in the woods behind our house.

A third and final tremor brought us to our knees. A sharp crack like a dry branch snapping in two was followed by a muffled roar that built to a crescendo, then died away leaving just the echo of our cries.

'What da fuck was dat?' said Jag, standing up and brushing himself down.

'There's no need to swear,' said Amina.

Jag was about to assure her there was every reason when Daniel cut him off.

'Probably the Craven Fault,' he said. 'It's the cause of all the earthquakes around here. It's nothing to worry about.'

'Oh My God!' cried Naomi.

We turned to look. She pointed towards the tunnel into which Matt had disappeared. Only there was no tunnel, just a pile of rock and a trickle of water seeping out to form a pool on the chamber floor. Her hand went to her mouth, and her legs gave way.

Devon caught her as she fell.

Chapter 4

All the blood seemed to have drained from my body. My teeth were clamped shut, I felt unbearably cold, and my hands were shaking uncontrollably. I would have fallen too, but Charlie was clinging to me like a limpet.

Jag was swearing continuously like a bad case of Tourette's. Devon was leaning over Naomi trying to rouse her. Daniel appeared to be taking stock. He came over and put one arm around me and the other around Charlie.

'We're going to be alright,' he said with as much conviction as he could muster. He leant closer and whispered. 'You've got to be brave Grace, for the sake of the others. I'm counting on you.'

He sounded like my father, and felt like an older brother. It was what I needed to get through this moment of panic

'Why don't you take Charlie over there, sit yourselves down, and check that he's alright.' He pointed to a hollow in the side wall to our right. It was a command, not a question, and I was glad of it.

Charlie came meekly, and we huddled together for warmth and mutual support. Amina was the first to join us, followed swiftly by Jag whose mouth had finally run out of steam. In the harsh white light of our

LEDs he looked as pale as a ghost. Naomi had finally stirred. Devon and Daniel had one of her arms over each of their shoulders and walked her slowly towards us. Either one of them could have easily scooped her up like a feather, but I guess it was better for her self esteem this way. They gently lowered her between Amina and me, and then sat down.

I had stopped shaking, my jaw had relaxed, and heat was slowly seeping back into my body, but my heart was racing like train. Jag had started muttering to himself, and Charlie, nestling into my armpit, was softly whimpering. Amina snaked an arm around his shoulders and rested it on my back. It felt warm and reassuring.

My eyes were drawn, against my will, to the ever widening expanse of water bleeding from that pile of boulders. I could tell from the concentration of light on that place that I was not the only one. I knew that we were all thinking the same things, imagining the same horrors, trying to blot them from our minds.

Daniel's voice cut through the silence like a knife.

'We have to stay calm, and decide what to do.'

'Let people know we're here, and we're safe,' said Devon. 'That's what we've got to do.'

'How the hell we goin' to do that?' Said Jag dismissively.

The fact that he had dropped his street slang told me just how frightened he was.

'I'm onto it,' Devon told him, holding up his mobile phone.'

'You'll never get a signal,' said Daniel.

'That's why Miss Walsh told us to leave them on the minibus,' Amina agreed. 'She said they wouldn't work, and we'd only lose them scrabbling around in the dark.'

There was an uncomfortable silence at the mention of Miss Walsh. It was as though we had made an unspoken agreement not to mention any of the others, in the forlorn hope that in doing so we could avoid thinking about what might have happened to them.

'It's worth a try,' said Devon.

In the blue glow of his mobile's screen I could see his face screwed up in concentration as his fingers flew across the keys. He shook his head despairingly.

'It's no good. I can't even send a text.'

'Nor me.'

I had forgotten about Naomi. She held up her mobile for us all to see. 'Daniel's right. There's no signal.'

'Why did you bring it?' Asked Amina.

'What does it matter why we brought them?' said Devon.

'I just wondered.'

'To take photos,' said Naomi softly. 'That's why I brought mine.'

'Good thinking girl,' said Jag. 'You gonna get some seee-rious bread for those pics when we get out of 'ere.'

I couldn't tell if he was being serious, or sarcastic, or using humour to cover his nerves.

'Better save your batteries,' Daniel told them. 'You'll need them when we find a way out.'

'I've had a thought,' I said. 'Maybe there's a radio in Matt's pack. Didn't he take it off before he went to help Wesley?'

Seven sets of beams probed in vain the pile of rocks where the tunnel entrance had been. Daniel stood.

'It must under there somewhere,' he said. 'I'll have a look.'

'I'll come too,' said Devon.

'And me,' said Jag, hurrying after them.

Their shadows slid along the floor of the cave and slithered up the limestone walls. Heedless of the water inching up the sides of their boots they bent to the task. Devon, as the strongest, stood halfway up the pile removing the pieces of stone above him and handing them down to Daniel who passed them on to Jag to stack on the ground. It looked like it was going to take forever.

'I'm sure he put it down on his right,' I told them. 'So it wouldn't be in the way when he came back out. Why don't you shift the ones on the left to the right instead of trying to move the entire stack?'

'We know what we're doing,' said Jag.

Daniel wasn't so sure. 'She's right,' he said.

'What do girls know?' sneered Jag.

Devon, however, had already shifted his position and he and Daniel were working from left to right.

Five minutes later I was beginning to wonder if I had made a mistake. The right hand side of the pile looked like a cheese that had been eaten into; Devon and Daniel stood perilously close to the rim of the concave hollow that hung precariously above Jag.

'I've found it!' shouted Jag, pointing to a strap protruding from the stack beside his feet.

'Don't touch it!' shouted Daniel.

But Jag had already yanked it free. There was a sound like walnuts being crushed and then, almost in slow motion, the stack began to collapse. Daniel had the presence of mind to dive to his left and slide down the solid half. Devon, taken by surprise, lost his footing and found himself propelled downwards by the collapsing pile into the pool of water at the bottom. Jag stood clutching the pack. Daniel hurried to help Devon.

'Are you alright?' he said clasping one arm and pulling him to his feet.

Devon let out a groan and hobbled away from the pool favouring his left leg

'I think I've twisted my ankle,' he moaned.

'I've got it,' proclaimed Jag, holding Matt's pack up triumphantly, oblivious to Devon's predicament.

'And look at the trouble you've caused,' Daniel replied barely holding back his anger.

Jag was unrepentant. Worse than that, it was clear he thought himself the injured party.

'Don't diss me man,' he said. 'It was an accident.'

Ignoring him, Daniel offered Devon his shoulder to lean on, and together they came to join us.

'Are you sure you've only sprained it?' I asked.

Devon winced as he lowered himself gingerly to the ground. 'I only know that it hurts like hell.'

'You'd better let me take your boot off and have a look,' said Daniel.

'I would not do that,' advised Amina. 'It will certainly swell up and he will never be able to get his boot on again.'

'That's right,' I agreed. 'Remember what they told us when we did that St John's Ambulance first aid course?'

'*We* haven't done it yet,' said Daniel.

'They said remember RICE: rest, ice, compression

and elevation for a bruise or sprain. His boot is acting as compression.

'We haven't got any ice,' Devon observed.

Amina pointed towards the northern end of the cave. 'I'm sure that water is almost as cold as ice.'

'Good thinking,' said Daniel. 'Come on, help me to get him over there.'

'Can you stay with Charlie?' I asked Amina. I was beginning to worry about the way in which he was becoming dependent on me.

'Of course. You go.' She moved her arm from behind my back, curled it around his shoulders, and gently eased him towards her. 'Come on Charlie,' she said. 'I need you to help me remove my back pack. I can't reach the fastener.'

'What shall I do with this?' asked Jag holding up Matt's pack.

'Follow us and bring it with you,' said Daniel. 'There may be some first aid stuff inside.'

I took one of Devon's arms, Daniel the other, and the four of us made our way over to the water's edge. Gently, we set him down on the floor sideways on, then lowered his foot into the pool. His body jerked backwards against me, and he took a deep breath.

I trailed my hand in the water. It was icy cold, just as Amina had predicted.

'How long do I have to keep it in there?' he asked. 'It's already going numb.'

'As long as possible,' I told him. 'And numb is good. At least you won't be feeling any pain.'

'I don't call that elevation,' said Jag unhelpfully.

Daniel reached out and grabbed Matt's pack. 'Give it to me,' he said.

Jag hesitated for a heartbeat, thought better of it, and let go. Daniel crouched, and carefully removed the contents one by one. There was what looked like a standard ration pack; a small stainless steel vacuum flask; a spare water bottle; a first aid kit; one of those super absorbent towels swimmers use; a Viper lamp like the one on Matt's helmet; a yellow and black coil of rope complete with metal ascenders and descenders; a shiny metallic thermal blanket; an emergency wand; a wooden pencil and a small pad of white paper; a black plastic whistle.

'No radio,' Devon observed.

'I think he had it strapped on his belt,' I said.

'Anyway, it probably wouldn't have worked this far down,' said Devon.

'Then why would he bother to bring it with him?' said Jag.

'Because we weren't always this deep were we?' snapped Daniel whose patience was wearing thin. 'Let's not worry about that. The other group will already have raised the alarm.'

'What if they're trapped too?' said Devon, voicing exactly what I was thinking.'

'Then the minibus drivers will hear it,' said Daniel determined to remain positive. 'Either way it'll only be a matter of time before the rescue party get us out.'

'How *much* time?' Jag asked miserably.

'Don't be stupid...how's he supposed to know?' Devon replied.

'It's not going to help if we start calling each other names,' I counselled.

'It helps me,' said Devon. 'Can I take my foot out now?'

I made him keep it there for another five minutes, by which time his teeth were beginning to chatter, and I was more concerned about him developing hypothermia than about his ankle. I had rolled up the leg of his oversuit, and was using the towel to dry his sock where it emerged from the top of his boot when he grabbed my arm with one hand and pointed with the other.

'The water level. It's rising,'

Ten minutes ago we had to lower his foot at least six inches to reach the water. Now it was level with the cavern floor and beginning to lap over.

'Where's it coming from?' Daniel asked as we helped Devon away from the edge. 'I don't see any waterfall.'

'That wasn't there when we arrived.' Jag pointed to the centre of the pool where the surface bubbled, with ripples radiating outwards in a circle that distorted the reflection like a cracked mirror.

'The earthquake must have diverted a watercourse,' said Daniel.

'Whatever. We can't stay here.' Jag pointed out.

'He's right,' I told them. 'Not if it's rising this fast.'

Desperate to find some higher ground, we looked around. The only possible answer lay on the opposite bank of the pool; on that shelf four metres above the water level, and the cave beyond it.

'We is never gonna get 'cross dat,' said Jag despairingly. The way he kept slipping in and out of street speak was beginning to get to me too.

'We go round it,' said Daniel pointing to the concave curtain of limestone on the western bank.

'I'll never manage that. Not with this ankle,' Devon complained.

'Of course you can. We'll help you,' said Daniel confidently. He waved Amina, Naomi and Charlie over. 'Come on you lot, we're getting out of here.'

I hoped that he was right.

From somewhere deep inside my brain doubt wormed its way to the surface.

Chapter 5

Up close, the pinkish curtain of near translucent limestone had the texture of a sea urchin shell. Our hands and boots found sufficient purchase on the rough surface to enable us to shuffle sideways on our bellies a few inches at a time. Daniel and Jag went first, sandwiching Devon between them. Amina came next with Charlie. Naomi and I brought up the rear. It took ten minutes for all of us to get across. My hands were badly scratched, and the knee pads of my oversuit badly scuffed. I didn't care. It felt like a small victory.

The floor of our new home shelved gently down to the water's edge. What had appeared like a ledge was far more substantial, extending backwards into a cave five metres wide, two metres in height, which led off to the left, curving away out of range of our head lamps.

'First things first,' said Daniel who had slipped unchallenged into the role of leader. 'I suggest that we check out this cave to see if there's a way out. But we can't all go together. Some of us should stay here.'

'I am happy to stay with Charlie,' Amina offered.

'I'm not going anywhere, obviously,' said Devon.

'D'yu got a 'nuver tink comin' if'n d'you tink me be stayin' here,' Proclaimed Jag

'For God's sake give it a rest Jag,' said Devon.

'God ain't nuffin' to do wid it,' he responded. 'If there be a God we wun't be in dis shit hole.'

'Wanksta!' Devon threw back at him.

'Cut it out both of you,' said Daniel. 'Jag I want you along.' He turned to me. 'What about you Grace?'

Momentarily the beam from his helmet blinded me. I put my hand up to shield my eyes.

'I'm sorry,' he said.

'That's alright,' I told him. 'I'd like to come.'

The ground was uneven and littered with rocks. Stalactites appeared without warning, some of them large enough to sweep us from our feet. For our own safety we had to constantly switch our headlamps from floor to ceiling. Then we realised that if Daniel picked out the floor, Jag the roof, and me the walls, we had it all covered. The width of the beams was such that doing it like that the entire passageway was illuminated. Picking our way over boulders and changing levels we made slow progress.

Two minutes in, we came to a section where the floor dipped, and the centre had collapsed, leaving a hole a metre in diameter. We shone our torches down and could see nothing but the sides of the limestone tube fading into darkness. In the distance we could hear the unmistakable roar of an underground stream cascading over a waterfall.

'That's Leck Beck dropping through one of those fourteen sink holes they told us about,' Daniel observed.

We stayed there for a while, listening in silence as the water hurried purposefully on towards Leck Beck

Head where it would burst out onto the open moorland. I knew he was thinking the same thing as me. If only we could get down there on a rope, and follow the stream to freedom. If only it was that simple.

The passageway climbed steadily until it opened out into a roughly circular cave five or so metres in diameter. The surfaces were smooth, as though they had been carved by hand and rubbed with a whetstone. It was easy to imagine how millions of years of running water tumbling pebbles over and over the rock would had created this effect. Two small openings on opposite sides of the cave were entrances to tunnels down which we would have to crawl on hands and knees.

'There's no point in all of us going down each of these in turn,' said Daniel. 'I think one of us should stay here while two of us explore the first one.'

'How 'bout d'yu take one an' I take de uver innit?' said Jag.

Daniel turned on him, shining the ultra bright beam from his 1watt LED directly into his face. Jag shielded his eyes with his arm and shrank back. It was as though the light was pinning him to the wall.

'I'm going to say this only once...' There was a quiet venom to his voice of which I would never have imagined him capable. '...while there's just you, and me, and Grace here. How about *you* stop this pathetic gangsta drivel for once and for all. You're not on the street, you're not a gangster, and your false bravado isn't helping; it's seriously pissing us all off. We're *all* scared and it doesn't hurt to admit it. If we're going to get through this we need to pull together. Do you understand?'

From behind the shield of his arm Jag nodded.

'We want to hear you say it,' said Daniel, co-opting me into his tirade.

'I understand,' Jag muttered.

'We can't hear you,' Daniel repeated.

I felt uncomfortable. Like a reluctant bully. I reached out and placed a hand on Daniel's arm.

'Enough,' I said.

He shook himself free. 'We can't hear you!' He persisted.

'I Understand!' Jag yelled. He twisted his body away from the beam, tripped over his own boot, and fell heavily to ground.

As I bent down to help him he shook me off, scrabbling against the sides of the cave to haul himself up. I could have sworn that he was crying.

'Right,' said Daniel as though nothing had happened. 'Jag, you and I will take this left hand tunnel first. Will you be OK waiting here Grace?'

He wasn't being sexist, not like Jag. I knew he wanted to take Jag to keep an eye on him

'I'll be OK,' I said. 'How are you going to mark your path?'

Because we had come through a single tunnel, without junctions or turn offs, I knew we would have no problem finding our way back. But there was no telling where they might end up.

'We'll do what Matt showed us and use pebbles or pieces of rock,' he replied.

I looked around at the empty floor of the cave. 'What if there aren't any?'

'Then we'll scratch an arrow whenever we get to a junction. Don't worry we're not going to lose you.'

I was more worried about losing them. Well, Daniel to be honest. He was the only one who seemed capable of holding it all together.

I needn't have worried. They were back in less than ten minutes.

'That was a waste of time,' said Daniel. 'Straight as the crow flies, with a dead end that looks like it was caused by a fall of rock.'

He waited for Jag to crawl out from the tunnel entrance and slump down beside me.

'You look crunchy,' Daniel told him. 'Why don't you stay here this time, and let Grace come with me?'

Jag knew it wasn't really a question. He sat with his head bowed and his arms crossed on his knees.

Daniel took his water bottle from his pack and had a drink. I realised that my mouth was as dry as sandpaper. It was impossible to undo the clasps of my pack with the rubber gloves with which they had kitted us out. I pulled them off and discovered that that most of my fingers were white and freezing cold. I rubbed them together, wincing as the blood fought its way back. Daniel wiped his mouth with the back of his hand, and replaced the bottle.

'Here, let me,' he said, reaching across to release the clips. Then he took my hands in his and massaged them gently. His fingers were long, and smooth; the nails perfectly manicured, like a woman's. I thought them incongruous given the nature of our activities these past few days, and the masterful manner in which he had taken charge.

'My hands are hot because while you've be sitting here in the cold I've kept going,' he said. 'Don't

worry; you'll soon warm up once you get moving.'
He reached into my pack, took out my water bottle,
and handed it to me. 'Drink as much as you like.
We're not exactly short of water down here are we?'

It was all I could do to raise a smile.

We left Jag huddled silently against the cave wall.
After all, he wasn't going anywhere unless it was back
to join the others.

The going was tougher in this passageway. At times
we had to lie on our stomachs, using our elbows and
knees to propel ourselves forward; thankful for the
pads built into our oversuits. At one point the tunnel
opened up to provide ten metres of headroom and
offer the prospect of a walk-through where we could
stretch our limbs. It was short-lived. Within a few
minutes we came upon a substantial rock pile that
blocked the passage. It was topped by a large choke
stone wedged firmly between the two rock faces.
There appeared to be a gap between this stone and the
roof, but from below it was difficult to tell how wide
it might be.

'I'm going to climb up and have look,' said Daniel.
'You'd better move back a bit Grace, in case I fall.'

'It's not worth the risk.' I told him. 'Even if you
and I are able to get through there's no way Devon
will manage it. And we'd probably have to blindfold
Charlie and drag him up on a rope.'

'Thanks to you, Devon's ankle is going to get
better,' he said. 'And I think you're underestimating
Charlie.'

Less than twenty four hours ago I had been telling
Devon the very same thing.

'In any case,' he continued. 'If we find a way out we can direct the rescue teams to come and get the others.'

I couldn't fault his logic. Not that it would have made any difference; he was already scaling the rock pile. Close to the top his foot slipped and dislodged a piece the size of a football that brought several more down with it. My heart stopped for a moment as I watched him struggle to regain his footing. He looked over his shoulder and grinned.

'False alarm.'

Heaving himself up the final half a metre he swivelled his body sideways until he lay prone in the gap between rocks and roof.

'There's plenty of space up here,' he said. 'You should see what's on the other side.'

I stepped around the debris he had displaced and cautiously began to climb. It was less steep and more compact than I anticipated. In no time I was lying beside him on top of the choke. Our headlamps probed the space beyond.

'Wow!' I said. It's not a word I use that often.

The passage continued for several metres and then abruptly opened out into a chamber twice the size of the one in which Jag waited. From a sand coloured limestone floor, pitted with holes and clefts, ribbed concave walls swept up and inwards to meet a barrel vaulted ceiling. The bottom third of the walls were purple tinged. Amethyst, the colour of my birth stone. At the far end a dark pool of water of indeterminate depth deflected our beams, to reveal a narrow passage that curved to the left and out of sight. There was an awesome primitive beauty about it. But instead of lifting my spirit it left me feeling small, insignificant, and fearful. Daniel picked up on it straightaway.

'Are you alright?' he asked. 'You look terrible.'

'Thanks,' I replied. 'You're not exactly an oil painting yourself.'

He shook his head. 'No, seriously Grace. Your face is pale, and you're shaking all over.'

I'd had no idea until he mentioned it, but I realised that I was shivering uncontrollably.

'Are you cold?' he asked.

'I don't think so.' Now my teeth were chattering. I was scared. I wanted to pray but I couldn't find the words.

'Then it's delayed shock,' he said. 'Whatever, you can't just lie here. We should climb down, and then rest up for a bit.'

'I don't think I can. Not like this.'

He turned until he was facing me, and then without a word slipped his arms around me, pulled me towards him, and held me tight. My head rested on his chest and I could hear the steady thumping of his heart.

Slowly but surely the shivering subsided. My heart beat fell into line with his until they beat as one. I remember thinking that this must be what it's like for conjoined twins. Warmth flooded through me, accompanied by a feeling of calm. I closed my eyes and surrendered to the moment.

I have no idea how long we stayed like that, but I remember that I was disappointed when it came to an end.

'That's better,' he said releasing me with what felt like indecent haste, and rolling over onto his back.

'It's a good job Jag wasn't here to see us. God knows what he'd have said.'

I don't know about God, but I had pretty good idea. 'Thanks,' I said. 'You're a life saver.'

'Not till I find a way out of here.' He looked down at the reverse slope beneath us. 'This one's a bit steeper. It's as well I brought Matt's rope. Can you get it for me?' He lay on his side with his back towards me. I unclipped the coil of rope from the side of his pack and handed it to him.

'Do you remember how to fit the descenders?' he asked.

I'd only done it a couple of times, but it's not the kind of thing you forget, not when your life depends on it.

'I think so,' I said.

'They're in the right hand pocket I think. The ascenders are in the left. If we secure the rope with a loop around this rock, attach a descender each and clip them onto our harnesses we can use them as a brake. Then do the reverse with the ascenders when we come back.'

'But if they fail we don't have any prussic loops as back up?' I told him.

He looked down at the slope beneath us. 'It's a free climb though isn't it? We're only using these as a precaution. As long as we make sure we've got a foothold each time we'll be fine.'

I knew he was right but I was thinking about Charlie and Devon. It was not going to be that easy for them.

While Daniel made sure the rock he had chosen would support our weight I found one end of the rope and began to thread on the descenders. Then Daniel made a loop, secured it around the rock, and threw the free end over the edge into the chamber below.

'You go first,' he said. 'Then If I have to I can hold the rope and act as another anchor.'

'What about you?' I asked.

He grinned. 'If it holds your weight I won't have a problem will I?'

It was hard to take offence given that he weighed at least ten kilograms more than me. I slid the lower of the two descenders further down the rope, attached it to the karabiner on my chest harness, and gingerly lowered my feet over the side of the rock pile.

Daniel was right; steep though it was there were plenty of footholds. Nevertheless, I was glad to have the reassurance of my descender. I found a secure plant for my right foot and a good handhold for my left hand. Then I squeezed the handle of the descender with my right hand, slid it down the rope, and released it so that it bit into the rope. Flexing my knees slightly I let the rope take my weight. Satisfied that everything was fine I continued without incident all the way to the bottom. I unclipped the descender and steeped clear.

Daniel was already on his way down, scrambling like a goat with total confidence in his invincibility. Suddenly he overreached himself, lost his footing, and slipped a metre before he remembered to release the handle, and the descender cut in, leaving him hanging like a spider from a thread.

'You can't beat a double figure of eight!' he yelled triumphantly.

His voice echoed around the chamber, and down tunnels. I wondered if there was anyone else to hear it.

It took ten minutes to explore this chamber and several minor tunnels along its walls. Then we skirted the pool, which was only half a metre deep, and entered the tunnel beyond. The passage rose steadily for several hundred metres before coming to an abrupt end in what can only be described as an underground ravine.

Less than three metres wide, and over thirty metres high, it stretched out ahead of us. We carried on in single file, Daniel's shadow magnified on the wall ahead of him. It reminded me of the ravine over which they'd rattled in Harry Potter and the Philosopher's Stone.

A hundred metres in, a fall of rock blocked our way. Daniel's beam picked out a natural bridge some twenty metres above us spanning the gap between the walls, and beyond that a solid roof.

It's no good,' he said. 'There's no way out.'

For the first time I thought I heard a hint of resignation in his voice. Disconsolate, we turned back.

'What's that?' Said Daniel focusing the beam from his lamp on the left hand side of the wall of rock down which we had abseiled thirty minutes ago.

It was a rope ladder with wooden slats. I counted seven. The last one hung loose at an acute angle where the rope had frayed and broken.

'It must have been there donkey's years,' Daniel said. 'Nobody's used rope ladders in our lifetime. You can see why.'

'Should we take it with us?' I wondered.

'What for? Our ropes are a damned sight safer.'

I shrugged my shoulders. 'I don't know. I just thought it might come in handy.'

He thought about it for a moment.
'OK, as long as it's you that carries it.'

Chapter 6

Jag was where we'd left him. It looked as though he hadn't moved a muscle. He didn't seem the slightest bit surprised by our bad news. When we set off back he followed silently behind me like a ghost

They must have heard us coming because they were sitting up, like meercats, looking expectantly towards us as we entered the cave.

'There's no way out,' Daniel told them.

It was painful to watching their bodies slump, and the hope fade from their faces. I looked past them and could see that the pool of water on the lower level had risen steadily and was now several inches deep across the entire floor of the cavern we had abandoned. Devon saw me looking.

'I've reckon that if it continues to rise at that rate,' he said. 'It'll take six or seven days before it reaches this shelf.'

'They're bound to have found us by then...surely?' said Naomi. I was relieved that she seemed to have recovered.

'Of course they will,' said Amina squeezing her arm reassuringly.

'Until then we've got to treat it like I'm a Celebrity Get Me Out Of Here,' Daniel announced.

'Only no one's watching,' added Devon.

'And we can't get out of here,' muttered Jag.

Daniel chose to ignore him. 'We could be here for some time,' he said. 'They're bound to know we're here but they'll have to clear away the debris in the tunnel that collapsed, and make sure it's safe.'

'How are they going to do that?' asked Devon.

'I don't know. With shovels and explosives I suppose.'

'What if they don't know we're here? Right here? We could be anywhere in the system,' I said.

I could sense everybody tensing up, if that was possible. We were already strung as tight as a violin string.

'Then we'd better let them know,' said Daniel, quick as a flash. 'I suggest that we use that whistle, on the hour, for one minute every hour we're awake. We blow three blasts one after the other, then wait five seconds, then repeat until the minute's up. We can start right now.'

After the first two blasts he decided to change the waiting time to ten seconds because the first five were filled by the echoes ringing through the caves and down the tunnels. We strained so hard to hear a response that our ears began to hurt. I don't think I've ever experienced a silence so intense, so laden with hope and fear. When the minute came to an end Daniel lowered the whistle from his lips. It felt as though we had been inside a massive helium balloon that had suddenly deflated, hurtling us to the ground.

'Don't stop!' Jag pleaded.

Daniel shook his head. 'We have to be disciplined about this. We can't keep doing it over and over again. It'll send us all mad.' He turned to Devon, 'How's your ankle?'

Devon looked down at his foot and gave it a wiggle. 'A bit better I think. I keep putting it back in the water for as long as I can stand it, so it's numb most of the time.'

'You can probably stop that,' I said, sitting down beside him. 'So long as you rest it and keep it raised up.' I was worried that his boots might swell up and become too tight; cutting off the circulation and preventing the fluids from draining away.

He looked relieved and started looking round for some pieces of limestone on which to prop up his leg.

'Here, let me,' said Amina. 'Come on Charlie, you can give me a hand.'

I had forgotten all about Charlie. He seemed to be reasonably alert and moved freely, but I could tell that he was still in shock.

Daniel sat down beside me. 'It's time we got organised,' he said. 'Like those Chilean miners.'

'We're not going to be trapped down here that long surely?' I said.

'How long was it?' asked Naomi, her voice trembling.

'Seventy days I think,' Daniel told her.

'Sixty six,' Jag's voice informed us out of the dark hollow in which he had hidden himself. 'They was rescued after sixty six days.'

'They were a hell of a lot further down,' Daniel reminded him.

'Seven hundred metres.'

'That's over two thousand feet. We're only what...fifty metres at the most?'

'Matt said this cave system was over three hundred and fifty metres deep,' Jag persisted.

Daniel raised his voice, causing the others to turn round and stare at him. 'I *know*. But *we* entered the side of the hill just forty metres from the top, and *we* haven't gone down *that* much further have we?'

The silence was deafening as we waited for Jag's reply. It never came.

'Right,' said Daniel. 'Let's make a list of the most important things we need to do.'

'Get out of here,' said Jag

'Ration our food,' I said quickly before Daniel had time to respond. The last thing we needed was the two of them kicking off again.

'And water,' added Devon.

'We're not exactly short of that are we?' said Daniel.

'But how do we know if it's safe to drink? Devon persisted.

'Because it's the same water that goes straight into our reservoirs,' he replied. 'And in this case the sheep haven't had a chance to foul it.'

'It's full of chemicals.'

'So is tap water.'

'Not like this. Tap water's been filtered.' Devon pointed to the stalagmites in front of us. 'Where d'you think those came from? That stuff's going to build up fur in your in organs and your arteries.'

'Like in the bottom of a kettle,' Jag added helpfully.

'It takes a 100 years for one of those to grow a centimetre,' Daniel told him. 'I'm not planning to stay here that long.'

'We need to conserve the batteries for our headlamps,' said Amina.

'Good idea,' Said Daniel. 'We can start doing that straight away. Where's that Viper Lamp?'

'Over there.' Devon pointed to an alcove in the right hand wall where the contents of Matt's pack were stored.

Daniel gathered them up, and laid them out in front of us. 'Where's the rucksack?' he asked.

'I've folded it up, and I'm resting my foot on it,' Devon told him. 'It's the nearest thing I could find to a cushion.'

Daniel picked up the lamp and examined it. 'Does anyone know how this works?'

'I do,' I said. 'Make sure the battery is attached then switch it on. There are four settings I think; *Camp, Low, Mid* and *High*. The higher the setting the quicker the battery runs out.'

'I wonder why he brought a spare lamp as well as a spare battery?' said Devon.

'Who cares,' said Daniel switching it on. 'Let's be thankful he did.'

It struck me that neither of them had used Matt's name. As though it made it easier for them not to think about what might have happened to him, and the others. It didn't...not for me.

The stark white light flooded the cave, swamping the rest of our headlights. As he flicked through the settings the intensity of the light rose and fell.

'If you leave it on *Camp* I think the battery will last about three days,' I told him.

'Two,' said Naomi taking us all by surprise. 'My brother has one for when he goes hunting upstate.'

'What does he hunt?' asked Devon.

'Deer and bears.'

'Cool,' said Jag.

'Gross more like,' she told him.

'I bet he blinds them to death.' Daniel set the lamp down on a flat slab of limestone. The light reflecting from the roof lit the whole of our immediate area, and much beyond. 'Now we should all switch off our own lamps,' he said, reaching up to extinguish his own. We followed suit, even Jag, although his was the last to be extinguished. We were bathed in a soft, warm, golden glow; our world seemed to end where it met the darkness.

'Food, water, light...what else?' said Daniel.

He knew the answers as well as any of us. Like a teacher, he'd already thought this exercise through. I had the feeling that he was actually enjoying it.

'How are we going to stay warm?' said Devon. 'I'm freezing.'

'Me too,' said Naomi, hugging herself, and shivering as though to prove her point.

It wasn't actually that cold. Probably about 10 degrees Celsius, like Mr Wilson's Science lab. He claimed it was the optimum temperature for our brains to operate in. We all knew it was just to make sure we stayed awake. But then Devon had been dangling his leg in the ice cold water, and Naomi didn't have a scrap of fat on her.

'Good point,' said Daniel. 'The secret is to keep moving every now and then, and to huddle together as much as possible so we use our body heat.'

He really had thought it through.

Charlie nudged me. As I turned towards him he leant closer and whispered.

'I need to wee.'

It was loud enough for Daniel to hear.

'Nice one Charlie,' he said. 'Hygiene. We can't use the pool, that's for drinking and washing.'

'What about that place up there?' said Devon, pointing to one of the large clefts in the wall behind us.

'It's too close,' said Daniel. 'And it's higher than our pool. We can't risk it seeping down some crack or other and fouling it up.'

'There's that swallow hole we found above Leck Beck,' I reminded him.

'Brilliant,' he said. 'We can use that for ones *and* twos. Just have to make sure Charlie doesn't fall down it.'

I wasn't surprised that Jag found that hilarious, but I was disappointed when both Devon and Daniel joined in.

'Come on Charlie,' I said. 'I'll show you where it is.'

When we returned they were taking stock of the food and drink in their packs. Jag was guarding his stash as though his life depended on it. Naomi appeared to have only a bottle of water. Amina, Devon and Daniel had already pooled their own supplies.

'We're struggling here,' said Daniel. 'Let's see what you two have got.'

While Charlie and I rooted around in our packs Daniel turned his attention back to Jag.

'It doesn't work like that,' he said. 'Some of us have got a lot more than others. Naomi hasn't got anything at all. It stands to reason we've got to share.'

'Some of us *need* more than others,' grumbled Jag. 'Anyway we'll be out of here before the food runs out.'

'You don't know that,' Daniel told him. 'In any case it depends on how quickly you eat it. The rate you go at it you'll have none left before you know it. At least we can make sure we eke it out.'

He got up, walked over to where Jag was sitting, and reached out his hand.

'Whatever happened to the seven wise and seven foolish virgins?' moaned Jag, but he didn't stop Daniel from bending down and scooping up the meagre pile.

'Don't ask *me*,' said Daniel. 'Wrong book. And from what I've heard you don't fall into either category.'

Jag murmured something unintelligible. It didn't take a genius to guess that it wasn't complimentary. But the fact that he hadn't voiced it confirmed for the others that Daniel's authority was now complete.

'Four Mars bars, three Snickers, three bars of Kendal Mint Cake – one of them chocolate covered – five packets of chewing gum, two packets of chocolate covered peanuts, five packets of crisps, three rounds of ham sandwiches, and three of cheese, four Matzo crackers wrapped in foil, two mango and banana snack bars, eight and a half bottles of water, six flasks of coffee, three cokes, three apples, two bananas, a bag of liquorice Pontefract cakes, and a self heating Lancashire Hot Pot meal for one.'

Daniel sat back on his heels. 'It's not a lot,' he said.

'How we going to do this?' asked Jag. 'Naomi's a veggie, you're a Jew, and I'm a Hindu innit?'

'And I am a Muslim,' said Amina quietly.

Jag regarded her with astonishment. 'Is you?' He snapped his fingers triumphantly in Daniel's direction. 'There you go then man. Can't just divide it all by six.'

To Daniel's credit he allowed him to enjoy his little victory.

'You're right Jag,' he said. 'Let's work this out together.'

Five minutes later we each had our own little hoard. Mine and Devon's both consisted of half a Mars bar, half a bar of chocolate covered Kendal mint cake, one packet of crisps, one ham sandwich, a flask of coffee, and a bottle of water. Naomi had been allocated the fruit and muesli bars, Daniel the matzo crackers, and he, Amina, and Jag a cheese sandwich each. That left the Lancashire hot pot, chocolate covered peanuts, the bag of Pontefract cakes, and the remaining bottles of water as a central stock.

Jag had argued that since the Pontefract cakes were Halal they should be divided between Amina and himself. Daniel reasoned that since they were one of the few things all of us could eat they should be shared; the rest of us agreed.

'I'm starving,' Jag said. 'So I'm having something right now.'

'Don't forget, when it's all gone, it's all gone.' Daniel reminded him. 'You can't expect the rest of us to give you some of ours.'

Jag started in on his cheese sandwich. 'As if!' he spluttered, cramming it into his mouth.

I looked at my watch and was surprised to discover that it was quarter past four in the afternoon. We had been down here over five hours; three and half of those cut off from the outside world. In all that time we hadn't heard a sound. No shouts, no whistles, no sirens, nothing, just the echoes of our own voices, and the relentless babble of the water rising in the pool behind us.

We ate in silence. I demolished half of my ham sandwich and had a warming drink of coffee. It wasn't enough to settle my hunger but I felt better for it. I was putting the flask back in my pack when I noticed that Devon hadn't touched any of his food. He was curled up into a ball and appeared to be shivering. I reached out and touched his face. It was cold and clammy, like a fish on a supermarket counter.

'Daniel,' I said. 'It's Devon. We've have a problem.'

Chapter 7

His pulse was weak but steady, and his breathing shallow. When Daniel asked him what was the matter his reply was mumbled and incoherent.

'He has a fever. We should loosen his clothing,' suggested Amina. 'I've seen this with malaria; his body is trying to lose heat.

'His body is cold, not hot,' I told her. 'We have to keep him warm.'

'D'you think maybe it's hypothermia?' said Naomi.

A icy hand clutched my heart. I had made him keep his foot in the water all that time. It was my fault. I should have known. It only took a drop of two degrees in body temperature. That's what they taught us on the first aid course. How could I have been so stupid? I began to panic.

'Oh God...Oh God...what have I done? I'm sorry... I'm sorry.'

Daniel grabbed my arm. 'It's too late for that now. What do we do Grace?' he shook me violently. 'Tell me...what the fuck do we do?'

I gulped deep breaths of air, and tried to think.

'The thermal blanket,' I told him. 'You've got to wrap him in that.'

Charlie ran over to the alcove, picked up the package and brought it back. Daniel pulled open the resealable fastening.

'There are four in here. How many do I use?'

'Start with one,' I told him. 'But put something on the ground beneath him first. He's losing most of his body heat into the rock.'

'What if we use two blankets?' he said.

I could barely think straight. A voice in my head kept telling me over and over again that this was my fault. It was taking all of my strength to stop myself screaming. 'I don't know,' I said.

'Packs everyone. 'Daniel ordered. 'Tip out all your stuff and lay them down here. Charlie, fetch Matt's as well.'

We lay them down as instructed, then Amina and Charlie and Jag lifted Devon's head and shoulders while Daniel and I passed the shiny metallic blanket under his upper body. Then they lifted his hips and legs so we could slide it down to cover the bottom half. Then we folded it over his front and tucked the respective edges under his arm pits.

'OK, Jag, you and Naomi and Charlie take his legs while Grace and I take his shoulders. On the count of three we're going to lift Devon, then lower him gently onto those packs.'

He waited until we were all in position.

'Right then. One...two...three...easy does it.'

We stepped back and stared down at him lying there, trussed up like a turkey. He was still shivering. Every tremble caused the crinkles in the blanket to catch and reflect the light, sending silver flashes all around us.

'What now?' said Daniel. 'He doesn't look good.'

'We could light a fire,' said Jag. 'I've got a lighter.'

'What with?' said Daniel dismissively. 'There are only sweet wrappers and the packs Devon is lying on.'

One more deep breath and I had finally won the battle over my reptilian brain.

'I'm not sure it would work anyway,' I told them. 'His body has to warm up from the inside out. We've got to make him drink some coffee, and eat something high in sugar.'

'He can have my half a Mars bar, and Kendal Mint Cake,' said Charlie.

'We could start by giving him his own,' said Amina.

Daniel and Jag gently raised Devon's head and shoulders, and supported them while I poured some coffee from his flask into the aluminium cup. I tested it on my lips. It was too hot, so I blew across the surface; watching the ripples, praying silently that this would work.

Devon resisted at first, trying to pull his head away. I persisted until he took that first sip, and then the second, and finally finished the whole cup, and then a second.

Amina handed me Devon's Kendal Mint Cake and I fed it to him a nibble at a time, like a baby. By the time he'd finished off the half a Mars bar he looked exhausted. I folded the spare material around his shoulders into a cowl and bent it over his head, leaving just enough room for him to breathe. Then we lowered him into the recovery position. When he was settled I lay down beside him, tucking my knees in behind his and my right arm across his chest, like a pair of spoons. I didn't care what the others thought. I closed my eyes and began to pray.

When I opened them again I discovered that Amina was curled up on the other side of Devon, sandwiching him between us. Someone had placed a second thermal blanket over the three of us. My left arm had gone to sleep. I wriggled out from beneath the cover, and rubbed the offending limb until the blood flowed back. I checked my watch. It was twenty past ten in the evening.

The Viper light had been moved away from our immediate vicinity. It lay on its side so that the light now spilled out over the area of the cavern we had vacated, leaving us the half light you find between dusk and nightfall. I had a painful crick in my neck and my whole body ached from lying on the hard and uneven limestone floor.

I stretched and looked around. Naomi and Charlie were just a few metres away, side by side under a thermal blanket. Jag was curled up in the other one inside his alcove. Daniel was in a seated position with his back against the wall of the cave. They were all asleep.

Beside me Devon stirred briefly, attempting to adjust his position. I gently loosened the foil around his face and felt his cheek. It was warm. I slid the index and ring finger of my hand around his chin until I found the pulse in his neck. It was reassuringly strong and steady. He opened his eyes and stared at me.

'Grace?'

'How do you feel?' I asked.

He looked pointedly at his chest, and tried to stretch his arms.

'Trapped...like a sardine. And my ankle aches.'

'Good. That means you're getting better.'

His look was guarded.

'I didn't know I was ill.'

I withdrew my hand, and rested it on his shoulder.

'I'll tell you about it later. Go back to sleep.'

He lay back and closed his eyes.

I stood and stretched for a second time. I thought I'd heard my name whispered. There it was again, only louder.

'Grace.'

Daniel straightened his legs and beckoned me over. I sat down beside him.

'You did a great job there...' he said, keeping his voice down. '...with Devon.'

'It was my fault in the first place,' I told him.

'That's rubbish. You did the right thing with his ankle. It's not your fault he kept his foot in the water all that time we left them on their own.'

It was just what I needed to hear. But I was still not convinced.

'I don't think I should have given him coffee though. I've just remembered they said anything hot *except* tea or coffee.'

He brushed an imaginary speck of dirt from his leg. 'Why not? So long as it's hot. You said to warm him from the inside out.'

'They're diuretics. They're supposed to make you wee more. It makes you dehydrate. That can be fatal with hypothermia.'

'I'm not sure that's true,' he said. 'Anyway, has he had a pee?'

I grinned. 'Not that I'm aware of.'

'Is he dead?'

'No.'

He grinned back. 'It wasn't fatal then was it?'

I shuffled my feet nervously.

'Even so...I'm going to have to persuade him to drink some water when he wakes up; just to be on the safe side.'

Daniel pulled his knees up to his chin, and clasped them with his arms.

'D'you think they're all asleep?' he made it sound like one conspirator to another. Like he had a secret to share, or we were going to murder them where they lay. I looked at each of them in turn.

'As far as I can tell.'

'How do you think it's going?' he asked.

'What do you mean?'

He waved with his left arm. 'All this...us, trapped down here. How d'you think they're holding up?'

I wasn't sure how *I* was holding up, let alone the others.

'OK I suppose. Nobody's panicked.'

He nodded wisely. 'I know. It's a miracle.'

'It's mainly down to you,' I said. 'The way you've kept your cool... taken control.'

'I didn't mean to,' he said. 'It just happened.'

'I know. But somebody had to and it's just as well it was you.'

'You've done your bit too. Sorting Devon out. And you stopped me from losing it with Jag.'

'Like you said. Somebody had to.'

He smiled and stretched his legs out. 'And how are you holding up Grace?'

I had to think about it. 'I'm tired, stiff and hungry. And I'm scared.' It was the first time I had admitted it to myself, let alone anyone else.

'So am I,' he said. 'I'm terrified.'

Dumbfounded, I stared at him.

He sensed, rather than saw, the surprise and disappointment in my eyes. He looked down at the floor. 'Seriously, I'm pissing myself.'

'I would never have guessed,' I said. 'What are you frightened of?'

He scuffed the rock with his heel. 'That we won't get out of here. That they won't find us in time. That I'll let you all down.'

'That's never going to happen.'

He smiled thinly, drew his knees up again, and rested his chin on them

'How long do you think it'll take for them to reach us?' I asked.

He shook his head. 'I have no idea. It depends on how big that rock fall was, how far back it goes, where we are in the cave system, and if the fall has changed the water course in some way that will complicate things.'

'I thought we would have heard something by now,' I said.

'Like what?'

'I don't know. Whistles, shouts, drilling, maybe even explosions.'

'Explosions?'

'Mightn't they try to blast their way through?'

'I don't know. They won't want to risk another rock fall. And they might have to put supports in as they go along. However they decide to do it it's going to take some time.'

I looked across at the others sleeping in the shadows. They looked so innocent, and vulnerable.

'We've got to find ways of keeping their spirits up,' he said reading my thoughts. 'For as long as it takes.'

'And who's going to keep ours up?'

Daniel put his arm around me, pulled me towards him, and hugged me tight.

Chapter 8

By eleven o'clock the rest of them were awake. Daniel used Matt's whistle again. The silence that followed the final blast was every bit as devastating as the first time he had tried. Devon thought he heard something but none of the rest of us did. I persuaded him to drink some water, and he insisted on giving us back our packs.

'You'll need them as pillows,' he reasoned. 'I'm alright now, honest.'

I wasn't so sure. Outwardly he seemed fine. His pulse was strong and regular, his temperature had recovered, and when Daniel took him on several circuits of the cave to get his circulation going he was steady on his feet, despite an obvious limp. But there was no telling what damage there might have been to his organs.

'Don't know 'bout you lot, but I'm still starving,' said Jag holding up his packet of crisps. It struck me that he was seeking permission, even though he didn't need it. When no one replied he tore the bag open and ate them one at a time in quick succession.

'I should slow down a bit Jag,' advised Naomi. 'See if you can make them last. We have no idea how long we'll be here.'

'If'n I need anovver mother I'll let you know,' he replied.

'There's no need to speak to Naomi like that,' I said. 'She's only trying to help.'

'I don't believe dis is 'appening to me!' he snapped. 'I don't need no help, what I need's to get out of here.'

'How d'you think the rest of us feel?' said Daniel.

'I don't give a shit,' said Jag scrunching up the bag, throwing his head back, and tipping the remains into his mouth.

Devon sat up and stared at him. 'This isn't all about you Jag. We're going to get through this by supporting each other. You want to go it alone, be my guest. But go and do it somewhere else.'

I could see that had hurt him. Devon was his role model. He crumpled up the bag and petulantly threw it close to the edge of the pool.

'Pick that up!' said Daniel.

'Pick it up yourself.'

Daniel started to get to his feet. Devon stopped him with an outstretched arm. 'Pick it up and put it in your pack,' he said firmly to Jag. 'We might need it to start a fire with later on.'

Jag started to stare him out, thought better of it, got to his feet, and went over to retrieve the crisp packet. Then he sat back down in his alcove with his back to the rest of us.

Seeing him eat those crisps had reminded me how hungry I was. I began to unwrap my half a Mars bar and found the others had decided to have their supper too. As they finished everyone put the empty wrappers back in their rucksacks.

We took it in turn to leave the cave to use our designated loo. Amina, Charlie and I went together. We waited at a discreet distance until the person ahead had finished. Daniel accompanied Devon, insisting that he leant on his shoulder. Naomi said she didn't need to go. Jag had already been several times.

Devon raised the question of loo paper. It had been bothering me too. Amina came up with the bright suggestion that we fill our water bottles before we go and use them to rinse ourselves – including our hands.

'Only use your left hand,' she said. 'As we do in countries where it is difficult to obtain soap or water, let alone toilet paper. Then use your right hand to hold the bottle, and to eat with.'

It struck me that she must still regard herself as belonging to Somalia, the country she had been forced to leave, and that must be hard for her. I also found it remarkable that her English was so much more correct than ours. When she spoke her meaning was always clear, never open to misinterpretation.

When we got back Naomi was standing at the edge of our shelf, holding the Viper lamp aloft, and staring across the growing expanse of water in the larger cavern.

'He's lost it,' she said, over her shoulder.

Jag was knee deep in the water tearing pieces of rock from the pile that blocked the tunnel, and hurling them over his shoulder. The splashes they made reverberated around the walls.

'What the hell are you doing?' Daniel shouted. 'You saw what happened last time. It's all going to come down on top of you.'

He seemed not to have heard.

'We've got to stop him,' said Devon. 'Even if he doesn't kill himself there's no telling what he might unleash. Every piece he removes, the faster the water comes out.'

He was right. What had been a trickle only an hour or two ago was now a series of mini waterfalls springing from every fissure.

'I'll do it,' said Daniel.

'I'm coming with you,' I told him

Together we edged our way around the curtain of limestone, retracing our steps until we reached the lip above the cavern floor.

'Hold my hand,' he said.

Together we slid from the shelf into the icy water. It came half way up my thighs.

By the time we reached Jag he had given up removing the rocks and was beating the wall of the cavern with his bare hands,

'This should never 'ave fucking 'appened!' He yelled insanely. 'They should *not* 'ave brought us down 'ere! This should *not* 'ave fucking 'appened. Fuck! Fuck! Fuck!'

We took hold of a shoulder each and prised him away from the wall. Resisting, he stumbled, fell back, and landed heavily on the rock pile, waist deep in water. His fury turned to despair and he began to cry.

We took it in turn to dry ourselves with Matt's towel, squeezing it dry before passing it on. Jag had not spoken since his tirade, and neither had anyone else. I could tell that what had begun as a personal expression of despair was in danger of infecting us all. The mood of the group was sombre; it hung over us like a storm cloud.

'Right,' said Daniel. 'We can't just sit here waiting to be rescued. We need to keep ourselves entertained or we're going to go crazy.'

'I can't sing and I don't know any magic tricks,' said Devon half joking.

'You don't have to,' said Daniel. 'We've all got stories we can tell. I think we should take it in turns to tell a story.'

'What if it is one that people have heard before?' asked Amina.

'Not that kind of story,' said Daniel. 'One about yourself. One that only you would know.'

'Something we've seen, or done, or experienced?' I asked.

'That's right. Or heard about firsthand.'

'We should have rules,' said Amina.

'Like circle time?' said Charlie quietly.

Jag snorted from somewhere within his alcove.

'Why not?' Said Daniel. 'There's nothing wrong with that.'

'Everyone should take a turn,' I suggested

'But nobody should be forced to,' said Naomi.

Devon joined in. 'You have to tell the truth. You can't just make it up. And I think we should reveal one thing that makes us happy and one thing we worry about, other than being down here.'

'The rest of us should be able to ask questions,' Daniel proposed.

'But only when the storyteller has finished,' I added hurriedly. I could see people being thrown off course by insensitive questions; me in particular.

'And you don't have to answer them if you don't want to,' said Naomi.

'We should use Chatham House Rules,' said Amina.

'What is that?' I asked.

'We use them in Business Studies. It means we promise that whatever we tell each other in here, stays in here. It is confidential. We keep each other's secrets.'

It was a great idea. I couldn't imagine myself being completely honest if I thought it was going to be blabbed all over the school.

'And you can't comment on the storyteller's answers, but you can ask another question,' said Daniel rounding it off neatly.

Nobody had anything to add. I realised that Jag had not contributed at all, and I doubted he would take his turn when the time came. But that was his choice and he was entitled to it.

'Why don't we have one right now before we bed down for the night?' said Daniel.

It sounded bizarre; bedding down without a bed. And apart from checking our watches there was no way of telling night from day. It was already apparent however that our body clocks seemed to know the difference even if we didn't.

'OK,' he said. 'Who wants to go first?'

It was a no brainer.

Chapter 9
Daniel's Story

'My name is Daniel. I am Jewish. I live with my mother and father in Manchester. My father is a barrister, my mother is an accountant and she works from home. The story I am going to tell is about a man called Nicholas Winton.'

'I thought it had to be about you?' said Devon.

'Or something heard about first-hand,' Daniel reminded him. 'And anyway, it is about me. About who I am.'

'And we are not supposed to interrupt,' said Amina sounding like our Head of Year in Assembly.

Daniel calmly continued.

'About a man called Nicholas Winton...and my grandfather. Last year my grandfather died. For the previous five years he had been in poor health and lived with us in a self contained flat my parents had built for him. I helped my mother to sort through his things. Grandad was my father's father, but my father was too upset to do it himself. I didn't understand why, because they had never seemed close. Now I do.

In a small, battered, yellow leather suitcase under grandad's bed I found a scrapbook, a teddy bear, a small wooden train, and a faded photograph. Folded inside the diary were two letters. They were both dated the 1st of December 1938, and signed by my great grandparents. The shorter of the two was addressed To Whom It May Concern. I have read it many times. In fact I know it by heart.

It read: "Dear Sir or Madam, We cannot find the words to express our gratitude for your great act of kindness in taking our son Jakob into your home. You will find him to be a good, obedient, and sensitive boy. We shall miss him more than words can say, but will live secure in the knowledge that he is safe and cared for.   We would appreciate it if you were able to support him in the practice of his faith or, if not, then at least enable him to attend synagogue where others will do so. We pray that when this war is over we may be reunited with Jakob, and able to thank you face to face. If this is not to be, could you please ensure that the letter we have enclosed is given to Jakob? May the Almighty grant you blessings and eternal life." It was signed Miriam and Lebel Adler.'

He paused to drink some water. Screwed the top back, and carried on.

'The second letter was addressed to Jakob, my grandfather. It had been opened, and from the state of it I would say that it had been read many times. This letter was much longer and, although I can't remember it word for word, I do remember the gist of it. It must have been an incredibly painful letter to write, and an even more painful one to read. It made me think about all those young soldiers going off to Afghanistan who have to write their wills, and compose letters to their loved ones. Letters from the dead.'

He paused, I assumed for effect. On reflection, I think he was holding back his emotions. Trying not to let them show.

'They told him how his arrival, eight years after the birth of the younger of his two sisters, had come as both a surprise and blessing from God. They wrote of the happy times they had enjoyed as a family, and those occasions when he had made them so proud that their hearts were close to bursting. They praised his intelligence, his commonsense, his obedience, his honesty, and his courage. They said that they had left this world happy in the knowledge that those qualities would enable him to cope with life's misfortunes, to raise a family of his own, to leave the world a better place. They kept repeating how much they loved him, and would always love him. They said they would be watching over him. That one day they would all be reunited in heaven. I showed my mother what I'd found. She knew all about it. "Don't bother your father," she said. "It's time you knew. I'll tell you." And she did.'

He looked around the circle of figures, backlit by the Viper lamp, our motionless shadows papering the roof and walls of the cave. He had us captivated, even Jag.

'By autumn 1938,' he continued. 'Germany had taken Austria and moved into the Sudetenland; areas along the border between Czechoslovakia and Germany with a high percentage of German speaking people. Because of the action which Germany had already taken against Jews at home, and in Austria, many Jews began to flee to refugee camps in the rest of Czechoslovakia. My great grandparents and their children were among them.

By chance, Nicholas Winton, a twenty nine year old English banker turned stockbroker of German Jewish descent, who was supposed to be on a skiing holiday in Switzerland, was called to Prague by a friend of his. This friend told him that a group of Jews and Quakers had persuaded the British Government to allow up to 10,000 refugee children between the ages of 5 and 17 to come to Britain, through an operation called *Kindertransport*. But because Czechoslovakia had not yet been invaded this operation did not cover those children whose families were living or sheltering there. It was obvious that Germany would be invaded very soon so Nicholas Winton decided to set up his own operation from his hotel bedroom. By the end of August 1939 his efforts had saved 669 children. My grandad Jakob was one of them. He was seven years of age.'

He opened his bottle of water and took another drink; just enough to moisten his lips and throat.

'Jakob's fifteen year old sister Esther was supposed to accompany him, but there was a mix up over the permits and she had to wait for a train the following month. In the scrapbook in my grandad's suitcase I found some newspaper cuttings. One of them told the story of the last of the Kindertransport trains. Two hundred and fifty children arrived at the station in Prague, eager to start their adventure; all of them believing that they would be reunited with their families when the war was over. In London, two hundred and fifty foster parents and sponsors were preparing to make their way to Liverpool Street station to greet the children and take them to their new homes. The children never arrived. As the train left Prague, Germany was invading Poland and closed all of its borders. The children were never seen again. Their fate remains unknown to this day. Esther was on that train.'

He paused again, gathering his thoughts.

'On the day my father was to celebrate his Bar Mitzvah his father took him aside and told him how he – Jakob - had come to England, about Esther, and how his parents had died in the Theresienstadt concentration camp, and his other sister Vera in Belsen. He told him that from today he was responsible for his own adherence to Jewish tradition, law, and practices, and so he should know the heavy price that his ancestors had paid to keep those traditions alive. Then he told him that he never wanted to discuss it ever again.

Nicholas Winton didn't want to talk about what he had achieved. For over fifty years he told no one what he'd done, not even his wife. It was only when she discovered a battered old suitcase in their loft with a list of all the children's names, their photographs, some letters from their parents to him, and some of the correspondence and permits involved, that she discovered the truth.

I asked my mother why no one had told me all this before? It wasn't as though it was anything to be ashamed of?

"Because it was too painful for your grandad." She told me. "I don't think he's ever stopped grieving for his parents and his sisters. And your father understood. Apart from that one time he has never mentioned it because he didn't want to be reminded of it himself. You see it explained why throughout his childhood his father had been so sad, and miserable and aloof. His pain was too great... and the guilt."

I told her that that I could understand him being sad, but not his feeling guilty. I thought that talking about it would have helped. Isn't that what you're supposed to do when someone dies?

"Not always," she replied. "It depends on the circumstances. You have to understand that on top of the grief that he felt for his loss, he also had this heavy sense of guilt that he alone of his family survived. What's more, of the children who did not escape on those trains over a million were immediately killed because they were too young to work, or died later in the concentration camps. Some were chosen for appalling medical experiments which they never survived. Your grandfather knew all this and was never able to shake off the nightmares in which he imagined their fates and those of his parents, and his beloved sisters. Many people suffer from this kind of guilt: the armed services and emergency services; survivors of the 9/11 terrorist attacks; survivors of road traffic accidents and house fires. They call it survivors' guilt."

Daniel paused again. I thought he seemed embarrassed, and uncertain about what to say next. Then it struck me that we were survivors...in as much as we had not been crushed when the tunnel collapsed. He must be have been thinking the same thing, and wondering if he had reminded us of the fact. I consoled myself that we still didn't know for certain what had happened to Wesley, to Matt, Miss Wilson, or the other group. By now Daniel had pulled himself together and started speaking again.

'I was so affected by the story of my grandad and Nicholas Winton that I began to find out as much as I could about what happened. I began with the Nuremberg Laws in 1933 which stripped Jews of their citizenship, and Kristlenacht – The Night of Broken Glass on the 9th of November 1938 - when thousands of Jewish homes, shops and synagogues throughout Germany were smashed and looted, and the first Jews were put in concentration camps. I learnt much more than I had ever been told about the Holocaust in which six million Jews were killed, about the setting up of the State of Israel in 1948, the Seven Day War, and the Israeli Palestinian Question today.

What I learnt left me feeling angry, sad, and confused. Ever since I remember, we have been going to Israel every year to stay with my Father's second cousin and his family in Bethlchem. I play with my cousins, but we never discuss any of these issues, and I never really questioned or understood what was going on there. Now I feel confused and, although I can't explain it, just like my grandfather I have a nagging sense of guilt.'

He stopped talking. It felt as though he had lost his thread, or perhaps he was trying to decide what best to say next, or how much to leave out. His forehead was creased with concentration and there was sadness about his frown that made me want to hug him.

'You see,' he said. 'My parents are Progressive, Liberal Jews which means I suppose that I am. They are critical of the way in which the Jewish State of Israel has developed, and is behaving. But when I think of what my grandfather suffered, and the rest of his family...my family...and those six million Jews, I ask myself am I being disloyal to him and to them if I follow my parent's lead? I'd never really thought about it until my grandfather died. Now it's all I think about.'

As the echo of his voice faded I became aware of the murmur of water bubbling up in the centre of the pond, and the drip, drip, drip of droplets from the roof above.

Chapter 10

'Just goes to prove...bankers aren't all bad,' said Devon, when the silence became too much for him.

'Is that a question?' asked Amina pointedly.

'Alright,' he said. 'What happened to this Winton guy?'

Daniel looked as though he has just woken from a dream. He took a deep breath, and let it out slowly.

'When his wife found all that stuff in the loft,' he began. 'She made him tell her the whole story. Then she wrote to some of the addresses where the children had been sent to live. I think she managed to track down about 80 or so who were still living in this country. Obviously the papers found out. His story, and those of the children he'd saved, moved the whole nation. In 2002 the queen made him a knight.'

'What was the photograph of? The one you found in your father's suitcase?' Naomi asked.

'It was of my grandfather and his two sisters, and their mother and father, my grandparents. It looked as though they were having a picnic by the side of a stream, but I think it must have been taken in a studio.'

'That's really sad,' said Naomi. 'The only thing he had left to remind him of his family. No wonder he never got over it.'

It was a comment not a question but nobody pulled her up on it. Why would they?

'Don't you think your grandad would have been better off talking about it?' said Devon. 'Isn't that what you're supposed to do when someone dies?'

'There is no right or wrong way,' Amina told him. 'Different people deal with loss in different ways. Some weep and weep and weep. Some pray to their god. Some talk endlessly about their loss. Some burrow deep inside themselves like a hibernating animal, emerging only when winter has passed. So long as it helps them to come to terms with their loss it does not matter how they do it.'

Her voice carried authority. As though she knew what she was talking about.

'But your grandad didn't get over it did he?' Devon persisted.

'No, I don't think he did,' Daniel agreed. 'But he didn't have anyone he could talk to. His foster family were kind by all accounts but didn't know his family, and no one really understood what had gone on. Even if they did they didn't want to believe it, let alone talk about it.'

'I don't suppose he could talk to his god either?' said Naomi. 'Not after he'd let him down like that.'

'So much for the Chosen Race,' said Jag from inside his hole in the wall.

It was a brutal, shocking, thing to say. We waited to see how Daniel would react.

'Don't you think I haven't thought that too? He said. 'It either strengthens or destroys your faith.'

'Which is it for you then?' Jag wanted to know.

Daniel had to think about it. 'I'm not sure yet,' he said.

'It isn't just Jews who think they're the chosen ones,' said Naomi. 'The Mormons do, and Catholics, and lots of Christians, and some Muslims I think.'

'I know a Rasta who thinks he is,' said Jag.

'Bottom line...nobody is,' said Devon. 'It's all crap.'

'You're right,' Daniel said. 'If you believe that you are a chosen race then it's not something people can become part of when they feel like it. You either are, or you're not. My parents are Liberal Jews. They believe that anyone can choose to subscribe to Jewish beliefs and customs, and anyone can go to heaven. Just as Liberal Christians do.'

Amina nodded. 'And the majority of Muslims do. It says in the Qur'an: *Anyone who surrenders his whole being unto God, and is a doer of good withal, shall have his reward with his Sustainer; and all such need have no fear, nor shall they grieve.'* You can choose to follow Islam, and you can choose to follow God by another name, and do good for others in his name. Only disbelievers and hypocrites exclude themselves from paradise.'

'Like me, I suppose?' said Devon.

Amina turned to face him. 'That is not for me or anyone else to answer Devon. For my part, I believe that God is merciful.'

'I don't need his mercy.'

'Then you have nothing to fear.'

It was all beginning to get heavy. Then Jag butted in, and it got even heavier.

'You said you felt guilty. What was that all about?'

Daniel nodded his head in acknowledgement of the question. He looked suddenly weary.

'All that stuff I found out about my family history, about the holocaust, about the setting up of the State of Israel, It got me thinking about what I really believe, and feel.'

'Like what?'

'I'm angry that we Jews have been persecuted for thousands and thousands of years, and there are still people who deny the holocaust even took place. How can they do that?'

'It's easy,' said Devon. 'Some people still think the world's flat.'

'Is it though?' said Jag.

'Zip it you two,' said Naomi. 'This is serious.'

'Innit though,' he muttered.

'Enough already!' she told him.

Daniel wasn't fazed.

'I'm angry,' he said. 'Disappointed, and ashamed, when I go to Israel with my parents and see the wall built to keep the Palestinians out of land they used to own. The cages in which they are made to wait for hours just to make the crossing to work each day. Zionist settlers building on land on the West bank that everyone agrees still belongs to the Palestinians. And when I see all those people driven into Gaza like the Polish Jews were in the Warsaw Ghetto.'

'Sounds like what they did in South Africa,' said Devon.

'Apartheid,' I said.

'It's hardly surprising though is it? Given they're surrounded by Arab countries with nuclear warheads trained on them. They're only trying to defend themselves,' said Naomi.

'It's about oil in'nit,' said Jag.

'No, it's about religion. Fanatical Jews against fanatical Muslims,' Devon told him

'Extreme right wing Zionists,' Daniel corrected him.

'Alright, Zionists.'

'Against extreme right wing Islamists.'

'Whatever. If they're both right wing why don't they get together?'

'I don't understand why the United Nations don't do something about it?' said Naomi.

'Like they did against Iraq, and Zimbabwe, and China over Tibet?' said Devon. 'No chance.'

' 'specially when they're all busy selling arms to both sides,' said Jag. 'Hypocrites, the lot of them.'

Daniel rubbed his forehead. 'It's far more complicated than that. There are two traditions both of which believe in an eye for an eye and a tooth for a tooth. Once the fighting and bombing started the reprisals were never going to stop.'

'So is Devon right?' I wondered. 'Both sides are afraid...it's as much about fear and revenge as about land and control?'

'It's both,' said Daniel. 'They're tied up so closely together it's impossible to tell them apart.'

'Like it was in Northern Ireland?'

'Something like that. Religion, and power, jobs, and housing.'

'But they managed to solve that more or less by themselves?'

'I think the majority of the people just got tired of it all. The extremists lost so much support they ran out of steam. So both sides gave in enough so they could work together. I can't see that happening in Israel.'

'Unless their fear of what will happen if they don't compromise, becomes greater than their fear of what will happen if they do?'

Daniel had to think about that. Maybe I hadn't worded it that well. He looked directly at me, then nodded.

'I think you might be right Grace.'

'What makes you happy?' said Devon.

Daniel smiled. 'When we go on holiday every summer to stay with my father's cousin and his family in Bethlehem.'

'What makes you sad then?'

'That for centuries Palestinian Christians, Jews, and the Muslim majority in Bethlehem lived in peace and harmony together, but now they all live in fear.

'It seems to me Daniel that you see both sides of the picture?' said Amina.

'I try to,' said Daniel.

'And you think that both of them have some merit?'

'Yes.'

'That they both believe they have God on their side, when in fact neither of them really do. Not if they see violence, repression, injustice as the way to pursue their cause?'

'Yes.'

'And you feel sorrow for both the Jews and the Palestinians caught up in all of this?'

'Yes.'

'Then I do not understand what it is that you feel guilty about?'

She allowed him take up time, but Daniel didn't have an answer.

'Your anger, sadness and disappointment I can understand,' she said. 'But no one should feel a sense of guilt because of something that people of their own race, culture, religion, country, or even their own family, believes or does. You are a good person Daniel. Use your concern to try to make things better, in however small a way.'

I think we were all blown away by her wisdom and sensitivity. I know I was. Nobody could think of anything to say. Finally Daniel stood up.

'It's nearly one in the morning I think we should get some sleep,' he said. 'When you've all bunked down I'll turn off the Viper light.'

'Please don't,' said Charlie. 'Please.'

'There's nothing to worry about,' Daniel replied not unkindly. 'There's nobody and nothing down here but us.'

Charlie squirmed. 'Please,' he said plaintively. I could tell he was close to panic.

'It might be dangerous to switch it off completely,' I reasoned. 'Someone might fall into the water.'

'We've all got our own lamps,' Devon pointed out. 'We can use those if we need to go to the loo. And Charlie can keep his own on if he wants to.'

'Trouble is there ain't no brightness control,' said Jag. 'He does that he's gonna keep us all awake.'

He had a point. It was no consolation for Charlie. Naomi came to his aid.

'*I'd* prefer to have the light on,' she said.

Daniel wrestled with it for a moment. 'OK,' he said. 'So long as you understand that if we do that the Viper's only going to last another day or so. Then we'll have to start using our own lamps, one at time. We'll have to place them below the shelf and maybe build up some rocks around them so the light is deflected away. At best, that would give us a week of guaranteed light.'

'That's more than enough,' said Devon. 'They're bound to find us before then.'

It sounded like a question rather than a statement. Either way, nobody responded. You couldn't blame us. It would have been tempting fate.

It took ages for everyone to top up their bottles with water from the pool, trail to the loo in turn, and eat something from their private stashes.

I decided to have the last half of my ham sandwich because it was already curling up at the edges. I ate it slowly, chewing every mouthful over and over again like they tell you to in the slimming magazines. It's supposed to fool your stomach into thinking it's full even when it isn't. I can tell you that it doesn't work, at least not when all you've got is a half a sandwich.

I washed it down with the remaining mouthfuls of lukewarm coffee from my flask. I would have started on the packet of crisps but I remembered what Daniel said about a week of guaranteed light. Even at this rate our food wasn't going to last anywhere near that long.

He had placed the Viper lamp in a little hollow in the wall of the cave, just beyond the one that Jag had made his own. Then he'd built a little cairn of rocks that acted like a shutter preventing the light from spilling out sideways onto our shelf. The only light we had was that reflected off the water now waist deep in the cavern. It threw our shadows dimly onto the wall behind us, the edges blurred and dancing from the ripples on the surface.

One of those shadows was Amina. She had moved to the very edge of the circle of light. I watched as she used her compass to find the direction of the Ka'ba in Mecca, placed her pack on the ground beneath her knees, and her gloves where her forehead would meet the cool limestone. Then she began silently to pray. I turned away. I don't know why but I find it embarrassing to watch others at prayer. It's almost as though I'm spying on them.

Those few hours I'd snatched earlier on made it difficult to sleep. From the random movement around me I guessed some of the others were finding it just as hard. I lay there in the half light thinking about my parents. Wondering what they would be doing right now.

I had an image of that encampment of tents that sprang up around the place where they were drilling to rescue the Chilean miners. I couldn't see that happening here. Not on a bleak Pennine moor. Perhaps they were waiting at home for news. Auntie Mary will have arrived to start making endless cups of tea, I told myself. Father Ryan, our parish priest, will be sitting there offering prayers and words of hope and comfort until Dad is unable to stand it any longer and politely asks him to leave.

My best friend Rachel will be lying in bed right now with that photograph of the two of us we took in the Trafford Centre, crying her eyes out. I wanted to be there hugging her, telling her I was alright. And my Mum too.

No doubt half the school are still awake texting like mad and posting on Facebook, probably both at the same time. It was what I would be doing.

When I finally got off to sleep my mind was full of disturbing images. Of broken windows, piles of burning books, and people cowering in doorways. I could hear the sound of breaking glass, the crackle of the flames and cries for help. In Year 9 they took us to see Anne Frank's house in Amsterdam because we'd been studying her Diary in English. Those images of skeletal bodies piled up and waiting to be thrown into pits came back to haunt me. I began to run. A huge concrete wall rose up beside me. As I twisted and turned it followed, herding me in. Ahead I saw a gap in the wall and squeezed through only to find myself trapped in a cage with steel struts and metal mesh. The wall closed up behind me. There was no exit. The sides of the cage closed in, crushing me.

Chapter 11

Tuesday May 31st

'Grace. Are your alright?'

Amina was kneeling beside me, her hands grasping my shoulders. I struggled to free myself from her grip. She let go and knelt up.

'You were crying out so loudly we were worried,' she said.

I sat up. The Viper was back in its normal position and the shelf flooded with light. They were all looking at me, except for Jag who was still huddled in a ball in his alcove.

I felt like a dish cloth someone had wrung out and flung in the bin.

'I was dreaming,' I said.

'Hell of a dream. It sounded more like a nightmare,' said Daniel.

'Was Daniel in it?' muttered Jag.

'What time is it?' I asked.

'Seven forty,' Amina told me. 'Most of us have been awake for some time.'

'Thanks to her rantin' and ravin' said Jag.

'Take no notice,' she said. 'If you want to have a wash we are taking it in turns to use Matt's towel to dry our hands and faces.' She handed it to me and went back to sit beside Charlie.

The water was crystal clear. I bent sleepily with cupped hands to splash my face. A ghost stared back at me. Wild spiky hair, dark semicircles beneath haunted eyes, a shocked expression. The last time I'd looked like this was after the sleepover at Kelly's house when she produced a bottle of vodka. My first and only brush with spirits. My last sleepover ever.

The chill of the water, like a small electric shock, snapped me awake. I cupped my hands again, swilling the water around my mouth, brushing my teeth with my tongue, swallowing.

As I dabbed my face with the towel I noticed that where the pool met the edge of the shelf it was overflowing faster than ever, like a weir or a mini waterfall. In the cavern the water level was already halfway up the pile of stones from the rock fall down which Matt had tumbled. At this rate I could see it reaching our shelf within a few days at most. Suddenly I needed to pee.

Amina came with me. We used her headlamp. While I was keeping guard for her I heard the sharp blast of a whistle coming in threes. My heart leapt for a millisecond as my reptilian brain kicked in, and hope leapfrogged reason. Just as quickly, it slumped. If it carried on this way for exactly a minute, and then stopped, it could only be Daniel.

'Maybe the rescuers have broken through and Daniel is calling us back?' Said Amina from behind me.

I checked my watch. It was eight am. On the hour he'd said. Too much of a coincidence. I waited with bated breath straining to hear a response, any response. It was surprising how loud and clear those blasts were considering the distance we were away and all the corners and piles of rock in between. I could see why they used these whistles for distress calls. Out on the mountainsides they must carry for miles.

As the final echoes petered out I checked my watch again. One minute and seven seconds past the hour.

'It was Daniel?' said Amina arriving beside me.

'Must have been.'

She put her arm around me and squeezed tight. 'These things take time Grace. I am sure they will not want to take risks with our lives or those of the rescuers. We just have to be patient.'

I knew she was right. I also remembered what Matt had said about how long it had taken the Misty Mountain Mud Miners to excavate just a few metres of passageway. If the whole of the tunnel we had crawled through to reach the cavern had collapsed it didn't bear thinking about how long that might take.

'They will find another way in if they have to,' she said as though reading my thoughts. I had never met anyone as consistently positive as Amina. Right now that was exactly what I needed to get me through all this. I put an arm around her waist and squeezed.

'Come on,' she said patting my hand. 'The others will be wondering if one of us has fallen down the loo.'

Our laughter rang through the tunnels and rattled round the chambers.

'Was that you two laughing?' said Devon.

'If it wasn't, I'd start worrying big time,' said Naomi. 'It means there are either ghosts or loonies down here with us.'

89

'Already *is* a pair o' loonies if they think there's anyfing to be laughin' about,' said Jag.

I walked over to where Daniel was standing looking over the pool towards the cavern

'We heard you whistle,' I told him. 'We listened to see if there was any response from deeper inside this system.'

He nodded. 'And was there?'

'No. But Amina thinks they could try to get in another way if they find it difficult clearing the rock fall.'

He turned to face me. 'We've searched those tunnels together you and I. You tell me how they're going to get in.'

'If they could get someone up that tube that leads down to the underground stream then they could lower us down one by one.'

'The one we're using as a loo?' he sounded as incredulous as he looked. 'Aside from the fact that they're going to get a nasty surprise if they time it wrong, that tube looks like it's got sheer sides, and it must be several hundred feet deep.'

'It's not impossible though surely?'

He folded his arms. 'What's that motto on the wall outside the staff room?'

'Something about miracles?'

'Miracles we do at once. The impossible takes a little longer.'

'I can live with that,' I told him. 'So long as it isn't *too* much longer.'

He cracked a smile. It occurred to me that optimism must be catching.

'It's your turn to tell a story Grace,' he said.

A knot began to form in my stomach. 'I'm not ready,' I replied. 'Anyway how come it's my turn?'

'Because while you and Amina were off having a laugh, I asked the others. None of them are up for it. Not yet.'

'Neither am I.'

'Come on Grace. I've done my bit. Now we need someone to keep the momentum going otherwise none of the others are going to have the courage to join in. And without that I have no idea how we're going to fill up the time, and keep everyone distracted from how bloody desperate this is getting.'

I hoped none of the others had heard him. I lowered my voice just in case they were listening.

'I don't know what to say. My life is boring. Honestly Daniel, I don't have anything interesting to share.'

He shook his head. 'Nonsense. Everyone has a least one story to tell. Do you think I found it easy?'

I had no answer to that.

He walked past me and stepped into the centre of the rough circle marked out by our packs.

'OK everyone,' he said. 'When you've all had something to eat, been to the loo, and tidied up, we're having another story. Grace has volunteered.'

It was news to me.

Chapter 12
My Story

'My name is Grace,' I said.

I could see how the formal introduction Daniel had used created an artificial distance between the person they thought they knew, and the one I wanted to portray. It should have made me feel more confident, safer somehow. But it didn't. I was conscious of five pairs of eyes boring into me like laser beams, searching out the truth, filtering out the half truths, exaggerations, and downright lies.

'I am sixteen on my next birthday. I live with my parents in Whalley Range, Manchester. My mother is a social worker with Trafford City Council, my father teaches physics at the Ernest Rutherford Academy. We are practising Christians.'

'What does that mean?' said Devon. It struck me that his personality had changed dramatically in the short time we had been trapped. The quiet boy who rarely expressed an opinion was now one of the most vocal.

'No questions. Not till Grace has finished,' Daniel reminded him.

'It's alright,' I said.

'No Grace, it isn't,' he replied. 'You may be OK with it, but it could put other people off when it's their turn. That's why we have the rule.'

He was right of course. I decided to answer it anyway.

'We go to church at least once a week, and on special feast days. We used to say prayers as a family before meals, and when anyone we knew was sick – although we don't do that very often these days because it's rare we actually sit down to eat as a family. My mother is an Extraordinary Minister, and my father is a Reader. I'm a member of the church folk group. We perform at the services and church functions, and visit old people's care homes.'

I could see from the expression on Devon's face that none of this meant anything to him. Nor was it what he really wanted to know. Was this really what being a Christian meant? I could see another question forming on his lips. He caught Daniel's eye and thought better of it.

I had lost my thread now. To be honest I'd never really had a thread. There was no story. I was just an ordinary girl growing up in an unremarkable family. Except maybe that we were all still together. No divorce, no step parents, step brothers or step sisters. Maybe that set us aside a little?

I became aware of the drip, drip, drip of water. Of five bodies leaning forward to catch my words, each of them wondering if I had said something and they had missed it. The atmosphere was laden with anticipation. But I had nothing to give them. Still they waited. Nobody spoke.

There was a voice though, inside my head. *'Tell them,'* it said. *'Tell them.'* I fought against it, as I had fought to suppress it all those years. There *was* a story. Not one I cared to remember, let alone to share.

'*Tell them.*'

Still they waited, picking up the signs like radar, sensing my fear like wolves circling its prey.

'*Tell them.*'

I unscrewed the top of my water bottle and took a long cool mouthful. Playing for time. Digging deep to find the courage.

'*Tell them.*'

I screwed the top on again, placed the bottle carefully down, and looked around the circle. Puzzled faces stared back, with the exception of Amina's. Something made me stop when I came to her. Her eyes locked onto mine. They were knowing eyes, as though she could see deep inside my soul. She smiled, and nodded her head. I was standing on the edge of an abyss, with no way back. I tore my eyes away, took a deep breath, and plunged straight it.

'It was a Friday evening. My father was late home from school. My Mum needed something for dinner from the shops. I offered to go but she said she had to get some money from the cash machine outside the Co-op. She told me to look after my sister. She'd only be ten minutes.

Beth was in a foul mood. She wanted to go out and play with her friends but Mum had told her she had to stay in. I was watching the television so I locked the front door, and the back door, and hid the keys. She laughed at me. '*You don't think that'll stop me do you?*' she said, and flounced upstairs. I pushed the door closed, and turned up the volume on the television.

I don't know why, but I suddenly decided to try and make it up with her. I went upstairs and listened outside her door. I thought I could hear her sobbing, but I wasn't sure. I knocked on her door. There was no reply. I tried the handle but the door wouldn't open. She must have pushed her bed up against it.

"Don't be silly Beth," I said. *"Come down and watch the tele with me."*

She didn't reply.

"I'll let you have one of those chocolates I got for my birthday."

Beth loved chocolate more than anything except the panda she took to bed with her at night.'

My eyes began to fill with tears. I took the crumpled handkerchief from my trouser pocket and wiped them away.

'When she still didn't reply I lost my temper and shouted at her.

"This is stupid Beth! Stop messing around and open this door."

I rattled the handle and pushed against the door. I could feel the resistance as she pushed back.

"You're just a big baby." I said. *"Baby Beth...cry baby Beth!"*

As I stomped down the stairs she screamed after me.

"I hate you Grace! I'm not a baby! I'll show you! Just you wait and see!"'

I looked down and saw that my hands were trembling. I took several deep breaths.

'A little later, I don't know how long, I heard my Mum scream, and then she was hammering on the door. I jumped up and rushed to the door only to discover that it was locked. I ran back into the lounge, and found the key beneath the cushion. I flung the door open. Mum was kneeling in the drive sobbing.

A bag of groceries spilled out beside her. Her body was swaying back and forth. She cradled Beth's head in her lap. Her coat was stained with her blood.'

Naomi reached out and gently took my hands in hers.

'In a daze I dialled 999 and asked for them to send an ambulance. I told them our address, that there had been an accident, and that my sister was badly injured. I must have sounded really calm, really cold. You see I felt completely numb. I couldn't answer any of their questions about Beth's condition. *Is she conscious? Is she breathing? Are her eyes open?* I already knew that there was nothing we could do...that they could do. Beth had left us for good.

When I got back to the front door my father was cradling them both in his arms. He asked me what happened and I told him. He told me to gather up the shopping, take it into the kitchen, and put it away. He would stay with Mum and Beth until the ambulance came. I did as I was told. It was a relief to get away.

I heard the wail of the ambulance siren and went back to the door. A small group of neighbours by the front gate - too nervous or sensitive to intrude any further, and too nosey to go away - parted to let the paramedics through. While they examined Beth, my father ushered me inside and asked me to tell him again what had happened. I told him as much as I knew. The rest was self evident.

Beth's bedroom window was wide open. She had clearly decided to climb out onto the porch roof, lower herself to the ground, and then ring the bell. Just to prove she could do it. Like she'd said. It was only a matter of fifteen foot or so, but she had been unlucky.

She must have lost her footing...slipped on the mossy tiles of the porch roof perhaps, and landed head first on the concrete drive.

Mum wanted to go in the ambulance with Beth but Father wouldn't let her. He insisted that we all follow on in his car. He kept checking in his rear view mirror where I sat with my arm around my mum, trying my best to comfort her, and failing. Eventually he spoke.

'This is what happened,' he said. 'Your sister was sent to her room for misbehaving. She was told she was grounded for the rest of the day. She said she could go out anytime she wanted. Neither of you thought anything of it. Shortly afterwards your mother put her coat on, ready to go to the shops with you both. She went to the front door to check that the shopping bags were in her car, and found Beth lying in the drive.'

He checked in the mirror to see if we understood.

'But that's not what happened,' I told him.

'Yes it is,' he said. 'Do you understand?'

I looked at my mother. She was weeping her heart out. I couldn't tell if she'd heard any of this.

'No,' I said. 'I don't. It was my fault. I locked the doors. I hid the keys.'

His knuckles were white where his fingers gripped the steering wheel. His voice took on a hard edge.

'This isn't about you Grace. Beth is seven. You are only ten. You should not have been left on your own. Your mother is a social worker. This could cost her job. Do you want that? Do you?'

I looked at my mother again. I knew then that she had been listening, that she had understood, because his words had stung her. She had flinched as though a knife had been plunged into her heart. I stared into my father's eyes in the mirror where they waited for my answer.

'No,' I said. 'I don't.'

I eased my hands from Naomi's grasp and reached for the water bottle. My hands were still shaking. I knocked it over. She picked it up, unscrewed the top, and handed the bottle to me. I took two mouthfuls, handed the bottle back to her, folded my arms, and clenched my hands tightly beneath my arm pits.

'We never talked about it as a family again. We told our story to the doctors, to the hospital social worker, to the police. They offered us counselling. We refused. To be accurate, my father refused on my behalf. I sleep walked through the funeral and the months that followed. It was only when it came to the inquest that the lies stuck in my throat. As I stood in the witness box in front of the coroner and the jury I found that I couldn't speak. Not one word. I think my age must have saved me because the coroner waved my evidence accepting the written statement I had made to police. Either way I knew that it was a lie. A bad lie...a sin.'

Naomi reached out for my hands again. I let her take them

'I'm calling a break,' said Daniel. 'Give us a chance to stretch our legs. Let's say ten minutes.'

I knew what he was doing. I could have felt patronised, but I didn't. I was relieved, and grateful.

Chapter 13

It is surprising how fast ten minutes can pass. Wait for a kettle to boil, or good news to come in the mail, and you can wait forever. Something you dread, it's there before you've time to draw breath.

'I don't think you ought to feel bad about any of it Grace,' said Daniel. 'Your sister's death was an accident, and all that your father asked you to do was tell a white lie.'

'Is you being racist!?'

It was like someone had woken Jag up and switched him on.

'Is a white lie OK *because* it's white, or is it *white* because it's OK?'

'Because it doesn't hurt anybody,' Daniel told him firmly. 'And it has nothing to do with colour.'

'That's bollocks,' Jag retorted. 'What it does is protect the person who's telling the lie. What you're really sayin' is that a lie that don't really hurt anyone much is white, which means that a bad lie must be black. An' everyone know that black is bad.'

Devon rounded on him fiercely. 'You're talking rubbish,' he said. 'It's people like you that give us blacks a bad name. And you aren't even black!'

'The thing is,' said Naomi, who hated arguments. 'Your father shouldn't have made you lie.'

99

'He did it for my Mum' I said.

She wasn't having it. 'Loads of people leave their kids to pop to the shops just like your mum did. They do it all the time. I'm sure she wouldn't have lost her job.'

'You don't know that.'

'Probably she would have just got a telling off,' said Charlie in a voice that was barely audible.

I shook my head. 'I think she's suffered more because we covered it up than she would have if we'd told the truth. I know I have.'

'That's because you feel guilty. You still think that it was your fault that your sister died,' said Amina.

'It *was* my fault.'

'Like hell it was,' Devon retorted. 'You didn't lock her bedroom door. You just made sure she didn't go out of the house. If she had she could have gone under a car.'

'Or been picked up by a perv',' said Naomi.

'Or been shot in a drive-by gone wrong,' said Jag.

'You weren't to know she was going to climb out of that window,' said Devon. 'She could have chosen a ground floor window. It was her choice. Her mistake. Her accident.'

Devon is right,' said Daniel. 'If you'd been allowed to tell the truth you'd have come to terms with what happened by now. You'd have been told it wasn't your fault...by the doctors, the police, and the coroner. You would have had counselling. You could have forgiven yourself years ago. You have to do it now Grace. It wasn't your fault. If it helps, forgive yourself. But really there is nothing to forgive.'

I didn't know how to respond. They were still

waiting for me to say something when Jag surprised us all again.

'What happened to the questions only rule?' He said.

'Jag's right,' said Daniel. 'Does anyone have a question?'

'Are you aware that you call your mother your Mum, but you never refer to your father as Dad?' Said Naomi.

It came as a complete surprise to me, but it shouldn't have. At some moment in time I must have made a subconscious decision that it be so. Now that I thought about it, I knew why. All this time I had blamed him for not coming home on time, because if he had I would not have been left in charge of Beth. What's more, I had blamed him for asking me to lie. But Daniel was right. He was only trying to protect us both, Mum, and me. Telling the truth would not have brought Beth back. I still hated that I had lied, but I couldn't go on hating him.'

'No,' I told her. 'I had no idea'

'You say you're a Christian,' said Devon. 'What kind of conversation did you have with God when your sister died?'

It sounds like a really cruel question, but I could tell he didn't intend it to be. He was genuinely curious. He deserved an honest answer.

'I stopped praying after Beth died,' I said. 'I still went to church with my parents but my heart was never in it.'

'Why?'

'Because I hated God for letting Beth die. I hated myself for what I had done, and for lying about it.

And because I was the one who'd pushed her into to trying to prove herself.

If anything my parents became even more devout. The rest of the congregation rallied round. They wanted us to know that they were praying for Beth, and for us. They offered us support, and reminded us that they would always be there if ever we needed anything. I find it all a bit too much. Probably because I felt so guilty...like one of the hypocrites they keep talking about in the bible.'

'Grace, I know this is a silly question, after what you've told us,' said Naomi tentatively. 'But what makes you sad?'

It was some time before I answered. It wasn't that I didn't know, or couldn't bring myself to tell them. The truth is I realised that there was so much that made me sad that I didn't know where to begin.

'So many things remind me of Beth,' I said. 'Photographs, videos, her room. It's been redecorated, and Mum gave a lot of her things to our local children's hospice, but I can still picture her bed, and dressing table, even the pottery Jemima Rabbit she had on the window sill. When I see her friends in town I find myself looking to see where she is. In a shop doorway perhaps or somewhere up ahead of them.'

This time I managed to unscrew the top from the bottle myself, and drank with a steady hand.

'Worst of all is when I think about the life she had ahead of her. The things we would have seen and done together. The boyfriends, and husband, and children, she would never know. Uncle Walter said I should live my life for her. But what does that mean? It just feels like a massive responsibility. It's hard enough living my own life let alone working out how to live it for Beth.'

I screwed the top up tight and put the bottle down.

'I worry that my Mum has never been the same since we lost Beth. I know she still feels that it was all her fault. I've tried to tell her it wasn't, but she won't listen. I'm also sad that there's a gulf opened up between my Mum and my father, and between my father and me. It's not that we don't talk, just that there isn't the same kind of affection between us. Instead of comforting each other they focus all their attention on me. My Mum's become over protective and my Father is only interested in whether or not I'm on track for A grades in all my subjects, and keeping up with my violin practice. It's like they're investing all their hopes in me. Sometimes I could scream.'

'You and me both,' said Naomi, with such feeling that everyone looked at her. 'What about happy?' she asked ignoring our stares. 'Does anything make you happy?'

'School... most of the time,' I said, enjoying their surprise. 'Especially being part of the musicals.'

'Do you know why that is?' asked Daniel. Not because he knew, but because he was genuinely interested.

'Because it takes me out of myself I suppose. Because I'm being someone else. And the music. I like the music.'

'Has it occurred to you school might be a surrogate family?' Naomi asked.

'That's a big word. What's it mean?' Said Jag.

'Substitute,' she replied. 'Or replacement.'

'It's a stupid word,' he said.

103

'No, it's a good word. An appropriate word,' she told him.

She was right.

Daniel suggested we have a long break so people could stretch their legs, use the loo, and have something to eat. It was midday by the time we'd done all that, although you'd never know it. The same unremitting half light, and the constant drip of the water; but for our watches proving otherwise it could easily have been midnight.

I felt strangely lightheaded. Not just light headed. It was as though a weight had been lifted from my shoulders. I can't really explain it, but I'm sure you can work it out for yourselves.

Now it was someone else's turn. I had no idea who until Daniel called us to order.

'Before we have another story,' he said. 'I think we should thank Grace for agreeing to go second.' He grinned at me. 'I know you didn't want to. It took a lot of guts.'

He started to clap and everyone joined in. Even Jag, who tried to make it seem like he hadn't really.

'Before we start I'm going to blow the whistle,' Daniel continued. 'I know I haven't been doing it exactly like I promised, on the hour every hour, but I have a feeling if I do it too often it's going to get everyone down.'

There was general murmur of agreement. I could see where he was coming from. He got to his feet and walked to the edge of the pool, facing outwards towards the cavern. He put the whistle to his lips and began the first set of blasts. By the time he'd reached half way I think we all knew it was a lost cause. When the final blast died away you could have heard a pin drop. My ears ached with the strain of listening so intently. As Devon started to speak Daniel held up his hand to silence him.

'Shhh,' he said.

We listened again. Praying that he had heard something none of us had. After what seemed an age, his hand fell to his side, and his head dropped.

'Sorry,' he said turning to face us. 'I was mistaken.'

'Bloody right you were!' said Jag bitterly.

Daniel came over and sat beside me. 'Right,' he said briskly. 'This time we really do have a volunteer. It's Amina.'

Chapter 14

Amina's Story

'My name is Amina. It was the name of the mother of the prophet Muhammad – peace be upon him – the founder of Islam, my religion. It was also the name of a famous member of the sixteenth century royal house of Zazzu, a Nigerian princess. It is the name my mother chose for me.'

She sat on her heels, upright, elegant, aquiline, serene. Every bit the part. The reflected light caught one side of her face, leaving the other in shadow. Her voice, smooth as chocolate, like her skin, had a rhythmic quality that was spellbinding.

'I was born in Mogadishu, the capital of my country, Somalia. My father was a doctor, my mother a nurse. The civil war had been raging for seven years and Mogadishu was not a safe place to bring up any child, let alone a girl. When I was ten years old my parents decided that we should move thirty kilometres south to Webi Shabeele, the Leopard River region from which my father came.

He told me that the river rose in the Ethiopian highlands and flowed over a thousand kilometres to swamplands beside the Indian Ocean. His family had lived on the flood plain for sixteen generations. He talked of vast fields of maize, wheat, and sorghum, orchards and vegetable plantations, and of camels, sheep and goats grazing the grass lands by the river banks.'

She shook her head slowly, and with great sadness.

'The reality was very different. Our drive south was like a nightmare. Both sides of the road were lined with makeshift tents constructed out of branches covered with tarpaulin, sacking, sheets and blankets. Whole families huddled in these dwellings. Over three hundred thousand people my father told me. Underneath the trees that had not been butchered for construction or firewood sat men and women, still like statues, their faces blank with resignation. The air was fetid with the smell of excrement and rotting waste.

As we reached the outskirts of Afgooye these temporary dwellings took on the semblance of refugee camps. There were shops and stalls selling grain and vegetables, and a sign pointing the way to a medical clinic. This was the clinic where my father would later begin to work.

We were much more fortunate. My father's cousin had a large house on the outskirts of the town of Audegle; a former trading post and centre for the slave trade before the Italians abolished it during the last century. It was made of stone covered with cement that had been painted pink. The roof was flat, and there were bars at the windows. We had two rooms at the back, and shared the communal areas with our relatives.

At first life was not so bad. Supported by my father's clan he and my mother found work in the local hospital. I attended a local school and had four cousins of a similar age with whom to play. The household grew their own vegetables and had a field of maize and four goats. The surplus maize and goats' milk was bartered for meat and fish. We lived as well as we had in the city. Better even, because there was no fighting, and we did not live under an umbrella of fear.'

She paused to take a drink. The manner in which she raised the bottle to her lips, tilted her head, and moistened her mouth and throat, was as graceful as her every move. She was, by nature, what I had striven so hard to become in the ballet classes that my mother sent me to for four long years in the forlorn hope of turning a duckling into a swan.

She placed the bottle carefully beside her, and raised her head. Even in the half light I could see that her gaze was distant. Far beyond the confines of our little group and this cave. She had transported herself to another place, another time.

'Then they came. The Harakat al-Shabaab al-Mujahideen.'

The tone of her voice was harder, bitter, with a hint of defiance.

'There had been a battle to the north between the forces of the Islamic Courts Union, and the Federal Government forces supported by Ethiopian troops. The ICU had lost, fragmented, and many of their supporters had fled south to regroup. It was our fate that members of the HSM had chosen Audegle. They were young, reckless extremists, many of them illiterate. Their heads were full of Jihaad. The warlord who had been our protector had been killed in the battle of Baidoa. We were at their mercy.

It was the first day of the festival of Eid al-Adha. My father's cousin had obtained a lamb and had slaughtered one of his goats. In accordance with tradition, friends and neighbours less comfortable than ourselves had been invited to join us for the meal. By what some saw as a happy coincidence, the Feast of Sacrifice had fallen that year on the 31st of December, and our Christian neighbours had been invited too. There were thirty of us in the central courtyard.

The carpet was laden with food. In the centre were bowls of rice mixed with shredded lamb and goat, raisins and cardamom. Beside them were mounds of grilled lamb, goat meat, and chicken legs, plates piled high with sabaayad flat bread, and red lentil fritters. At each place a bowl of spiced black tea.'

I felt my stomach tighten, and saliva begin to moisten my mouth. Involuntary movements around the circle confirmed that I was not alone in having had my pangs of hunger roused.

'They burst through the doors, front and back. Tall, skinny, clean shaven youths, and several older men. The youths wore long green shirts and trousers. On their feet they had sandals. Bullet belts were slung over their shoulders. Their heads were covered with Keffiah scarves leaving a slit for their eyes. They pointed their guns at us. In some of their eyes I read anger, in others apprehension.

The older men were bearded. They wore camouflage uniforms. Cream turbans on their heads were tied in tails behind them. The boots on their feet were covered with dust. Rifles slung over their shoulders, they held pistols in their hands. Their eyes were expressionless as they surveyed the room. That they were in command was evident from the manner in which they held themselves, and the way in which the others deferred to them.

'Peace be upon you.' My father's cousin said as he started to rise. The youth nearest to him stepped forward and prodded him back onto his heels with the barrel of his gun.

'If you value your lives, be still,' said one the bearded men, pointing his finger in the manner that we reserve for dogs. He walked slowly around the outside of the circle that we had made, staring at each of us in turn. When he came to me, and stopped, I felt a terror I cannot describe. He completed his tour and stood with his hands on his hips. 'Cover your heads!' he commanded.'

Amina looked around our circle, meeting each of our eyes in turn as she spoke. 'You see we were indoors, and had no need to wear our hijab or a burqua. But these were strangers, and men. In his eyes those youths gazing upon our nakedness were committing sin. We, uncovered, were inflaming them.'

Jag shook his head in disbelief. Devon was bursting to say something, but had the sense to keep it to himself. She raised her head, stared once more into space, and continued.

'Those of us who wore a coantino – a cloth draped across our shoulders and around our waist – used that to make a head shawl. Others made use of their neck scarves. Our Christian neighbours were frozen in fear and disbelief. I think it was in part what he had been hoping for.

'You have Christians in your house?' he said.

'They are my neighbours. Our friends,' my father's cousin replied.

He snorted contemptuously. 'And you allow your women to sit uncovered beside them?' He pointed to our neighbours. 'You will leave now!'

They scrambled to their feet and scurried out, relieved I think that they had escaped a more terrible fate.

'You,' he said, pointing at my father's cousin. 'Will remain here. You will be punished. And, as is the custom on this Feast of Sacrifice you will be pleased to invite my men – as poor hungry strangers - to partake of your hospitality. The rest of you will go to your rooms.'

Nobody moved. My father's cousin's wife threw her arms around him in the vain hope that this would save him.

'Now!' he bellowed.

As people began to rise to their feet the youths moved in to pull my father's cousin and his wife apart. My father clasped me to his chest and led me away, my Mother beside us.'

Her voice changed in tone. It was as though she was trying to distance herself from the painful memory.

'We sat huddled together in our room listening to the swish of the cane, the thud as it landed, and the grunt of pain that he was trying so hard to hide, to spare his wife further anguish. I counted twenty strokes. Then there was silence but for the muffled sound of his wife wailing.

We did not know it then but this was the beginning of a new, terrible, chapter in our lives. Mujahideen had come to stay. Gradually al-Shabaab strengthened its grip over the warlords in our region and began to recruit young men from the mosques to swell their ranks. Worst of all, their interpretation of Shariah law became the norm.

Three months after they had burst into our house my mother and I were stopped on the street by a group of young men. They that said our clothes were non Islamic, because they were not thick enough. That we must replace them with a heavier cloth within three days, or face a beating.'

She smiled wryly.

'The place in the market where the cloth was sold was run by al-Shabaab. Not long afterwards our Christian neighbours left to head North. I found out later that two of their friends had been accused of spying and had been stoned to death. Over the next six months the violence escalated. Not only Christians but Sulfi Muslims also became a target for their hatred. There was a man in the centre of the market who wore a black mask around his face. People were taken to him if they were found to have gold or silver fillings in their teeth. While other men held them he would tear the offending teeth from their sockets.'

'Just like the Nazi's,' Daniel muttered.

She turned to face him. 'Yes Daniel,' she said. 'And yet not the same at all. Their justification was that the wearing of gold and silver, of any ornaments at all, was un-Islamic, showing as they did an obsession with beauty, and fashion, and with wealth. But this was the least of it.'

She turned her head away again.

'It was no longer safe for women to walk alone on the streets or even with their brothers. Unmarried girls were targeted. Members of the muhajeddin wanted to force them into marriage. If they refused then they were raped. If they still refused to marry they could be stoned for having committed adultery because they had been raped. One girl to whom this happened was only thirteen years old. And there were cases of women who refused to be married being beheaded, and their heads sent to their father.'

Beside me Naomi gasped. I felt a sudden chill although I knew there was no draught down here. Amina reached for her water. We waited patiently, hoping as much for ourselves as for her that her story had reached its lowest point; that nothing worse could possibly have happened. It was almost a minute before she was ready to start again.

'On the night before my eleventh birthday my mother slipped out of the house to collect a present for me from another relative who was too frightened to come out. She should have waited for my father to return from the clinic where he had been delayed, or asked one of our male kinfolk to go. But it was only two houses away, and she did not. When my father came home she had still not returned. He went with his cousin to look for her.'

She paused, and looked down at the limestone floor. She took a deep breath, gathered herself, and continued. Her voice was less assured, faltering.

'They found her the following morning. In a ditch, by a field of maize, two kilometres away. She had been so badly beaten that at first they did not recognize her. Although they did not tell me this themselves, I later learned from my cousins that she had been raped... many times.'

Naomi's hand gripped mine and squeezed it tightly.

Not for my benefit but for her own. It felt like she needed to know in a concrete way that we were here, safe, a million miles away in time and space from the horror unfolding before us. And there was something else. A recognition, a sharing almost, of the pain that Amina's telling of this story must be causing her. Amina raised her head and continued. Her voice was firmer now, as though a hazardous bridge had been crossed.

'My father was warned that the Mujahideen would be coming for him. To silence him and to punish him for allowing his wife to walk the streets alone. He decided that we must get away. For my sake, more than his own. His plan was to escape into Kenya and then travel on from there to join family in England. To avoid suspicion we took as little with us we could. I sat behind him in our car wearing a jalabeeb that covered me from head to foot. Each time we passed a group of soldiers or came to a check point I lowered my head. My father's story was that he was going to work in a clinic to the South. There was fighting close to the border and we had to turn back. We turned northwards. After nine days we arrived in the port of Bosasso on the northern coast.'

She lifted the bottle and wet her lips.

'It was a frightening place, teeming with people. My father sold our car and set about finding a boat willing to take us across the Gulf to the Yemen. It was not difficult. There were many people wishing to make that trip and many pirates ready to help them...for a price. Before he went to haggle with them my father made me hide the majority of our cash in my undergarments. It was not too much because his salary and savings were safe in a bank.

He spent four days trying to find a broker he could trust to take us to a boat where we would be safe. Safer that is, than in one of the many old and rotten boats run by evil men who charged only fifty to a hundred dollars for the crossing, and made up their profit in other ways. We had heard stories of people locked in dark rooms; beaten, raped, their belongings taken. Some of them never making the crossing at all, but ending up in shallow graves by the shoreline. In Yemen I met a woman whose children had been torn from her and thrown into the shark infested sea.'

She said it in a matter of fact voice; wearying of this catalogue of wickedness and cruelty.

'My father paid $500 for the crossing. Still we were cramped with thirty others in a boat intended for half that number. But our journey was uneventful. The sea was choppy but according to the captain remarkably calm. It took us two and a half days. So strong were the sun's rays that my face and arms were burned despite my jalabeeb. We saw several other boats and a tanker during the crossing, but were never approached by another vessel. We landed on the shore of Yemen near the town of Ahwar.

My father used his mobile phone to call a friend with whom he had trained who was working with a French humanitarian organisation -Médecins Sans Frontières – Doctors Without Frontiers. She came to pick us up and took us back to the clinic where they were treating refugees likes us.

My father told me that he had arranged for me to fly from Aden to England, where relatives would be waiting for me. But I must go alone. He would be staying to work as a volunteer with the Médecins Sans

Frontières. I pleaded with him to come with me, but he said he could not. We would be refused entry and sent back, whereas I – arriving as an unaccompanied child claiming asylum – would not. I said that I would stay with him, but he said if I did we would both have to register in Yemen as refugees and never be able to go to England, or return to Somalia.

She looked slowly around the circle once more, so that we could see the truth in her eyes. I felt that I was looking deep into her soul.

'That,' she said. 'Is how I came to be here, in England, with you.'

Chapter 15

Nobody spoke. Even Daniel who could always be counted on to say something was speechless. I think that we were all in shock. I know I was. Amina had joined the Academy in Year Seven, at the same time as the rest of us. From the start she had seemed so at ease, so together, so self-assured that it was difficult to believe that she had been through all of this.

She sat up and looked around the circle of faces. 'My legs are cramped,' she said. 'I need to stretch them. I am sure that you do too.'

With that she stood, turned, and walked slowly towards the edge of our shelf. She stood there looking out across the water at the slowly shrinking vastness of the cavern. The light from the lamp, reflected back off the limestone walls and the surface of the water, threw her into silhouette. Where it touched the edges of her head and body it shimmered like the corona around a total eclipse.

'Good idea,' Daniel said at last. 'And I don't know about you lot but I don't think I can take much more this morning. Shall we leave the questions until after Lunch?'

'Lunch!' Jag snorted.

He was becoming good at that, annoyingly so. Daniel was becoming equally good at ignoring his petulant outbursts.

'You know what I mean,' he said. 'I hope you're all managing to eke it out?'

Nobody responded. I knew that however hard I rationed them my meagre provisions would be gone within three days. I had a sneaking suspicion that Jag's were already exhausted.

'Daniel, I think you should see this,' Amina said quietly.

He went across to join her. Curious, Naomi and I followed. Jag slunk back into his hole, Devon, still favouring his ankle, leant against the wall. Charlie remained seated, head down between his knees.

The reason she had called us over was obvious. The rock pile where our entrance tunnel had been was now completely submerged, and the water lapped our feet on the edge of the shelf.

'Another day at the most, and we'll have to leave this spot,' Daniel observed, keeping his voice deliberately low. He turned to me. 'We can move to that other cavern we found Grace. It's higher up and far enough away.'

'How will we get Devon over that rock wall?' I said.

'He'll manage with his good leg. We can use one rope as a safety rope and another to lower him down. The same with Charlie if we have to.'

Neither of the others knew what we were talking about.

'What rock wall...what cavern?' Said Naomi.

'Don't worry, you'll soon find out,' Daniel told her.

'But if we leave here how are they going to hear the whistle? How will we hear them when they break through?'

I could hear the panic in her voice. Daniel reached out and took her hand. 'It's alright Naomi. Sound travels miles in these caves. And I doubt that they'll be breaking through over there.' He nodded towards the expanse of water. 'Not now. They'll find some other way.'

She pulled her hand free, turned, and walked away. Amina followed her.

I knew exactly what she was thinking. If sound really travelled miles why hadn't they heard us yet, and we them? And if they couldn't use the old tunnel then how would they get to us?

'That's *all* we need,' said Daniel.

I thought he was talking about Naomi but he was kneeling beside the Viper lamp. A small red LED was flashing on the side.

'It's the fuel gauge,' he said. 'It's going to run out anytime now.'

'You can use mine instead,' I told him.

'No way. I need you Grace. You know the way, they don't. I'll get Devon to lend us his. He can have it back if we start moving.'

We walked back to join the others.

'Where is Charlie?' said Amina.

'I think he's gone to the loo,' said Devon.

'On his own? He's never done that before,' said Naomi.

'Give him a break,' Devon told her. 'He's a big boy, and it's not as though he's never been before.'

'But that's just the point,' Naomi retorted. 'He's not a big boy. He's small, and timid, and frightened.'

She bent down, picked up her helmet, and put it on. 'I'm going to see if he's alright.'

' E won't 'tank you for it,' Jag said to her back as she negotiated the inner chamber and disappeared down the tunnel.

'Right,' said Daniel briskly. 'I think we should move off this shelf into the cave. It's only a couple of feet higher but it should give us a bit more time here.'

'I is not movin',' said Jag.

'Fair enough. You stay here then.'

I looked at Daniel. I couldn't believe that he would abandon Jag, no matter how annoying he had become. Daniel leaned closer, and whispered in my ear.

'When that water reaches his cosy little nest he'll move. See if he doesn't.'

The three of us had only just moved all of the packs into the cave when we heard the sound of Naomi's voice muffled by the twists and turns of the tunnel walls.

'What's she saying?' said Devon.

'It sounds like *Help*!' I said.

Daniel grabbed his helmet, and switched on his lamp. 'I'm going. You two stay here.'

'I'm coming with you,' I said.

Naomi called out again. There was panic in her voice.

'I'd come too if I could,' said Devon. 'But I'd only slow you down.'

'I know you would,' said Daniel. 'Come on Grace.'

As we entered the tunnel dark imaginings crowded my mind. Daniel bellowed as loudly as he could.

'Hang on Naomi...we're coming!'

Naomi stood with her back to us. As the beams of our lamps lit up the space she moved slowly to the side revealing little Charlie. He had his back to us. His head was lowered as though he was staring intently at something on the ground.

It was only when we stepped closer that I could see that he was on the edge of the sump hole, his feet more than half way across the rim. Another inch and he would be gone. None of us spoke. Naomi held out her arm warning us to stay back. Slowly she inched her way back to join us.

'He's been like this for ages,' she whispered. 'When I went to pull him back he edged forward until he was stood like that. I've tried talking to him but he doesn't seem to hear.'

I knew what she meant. We had been here before, Charlie and I.

'Nothing any of us says will get to him,' I told them. 'He's in a world of his own, like a sleepwalker. You know what happens when you wake a sleep walker?'

'They fall down stairs?' said Naomi.

If the vampire horror movies were anything to go by she was probably right.

'Only this stairwell is hundreds of feet deep,' Daniel observed sombrely.

I started to untie my boots. 'Leave this to me,' I said.

'Be careful,' Daniel said softly. 'We can't afford to lose you.'

I struggled to stay calm, to control my anger. Maybe I was wrong, but it sounded as though he thought Charlie surplus to requirements. I stepped out of my boots. The limestone floor was cool and rough to my stockinged feet. The sound of water rushing to join the Beck filtered up through the sump.

Charlie seemed transfixed by that deep black hole and river below.

I edged forward on the soles of my feet, like a cat anxious not to disturb a roosting bird. Within arms' length of Charlie I stopped and took stock. Did I speak and risk frightening him, or grab hold and pray that he did not fall forward and take me with him? I was worried that he would hear my heart pounding in my chest. The longer I delayed the more uncertain I became.

Suddenly I heard him sob and saw his foot begin to move. Throwing caution to the wind I flung my arms around him and, as he began to pitch forward, threw myself to the right. My head struck the side of the tunnel, and searing blackness descended.

'Grace! Grace!'

The voice was distant, disembodied, and persistent. My head throbbed; there was dull a pain in my shoulder. When I opened my eyes my vision was blurred.

'Grace, are you alright?'

It was Daniel. There was panic in his voice. Gradually the outline of his face materialized from the fog.

'Thank God,' he said kneeling down beside me. He placed his hand gingerly on the back of my head. When he brought it away it was sticky and wet. 'You're bleeding,' he said.

I pushed myself tentatively into a sitting position with my back against the wall.

'I'd take it slowly if I were you,' said Naomi.

She was standing a couple of feet away staring down at Charlie who sat curled up in a ball at her feet.

'How is he?' I asked, flinching as I discovered that the simple act of speaking made my head hurt.

'Better than you by the looks of it,' said Daniel. 'You cushioned his fall and saved all the impact for yourself.' He produced a handkerchief and handed it to me. 'Here,' he said. 'I haven't used it. Press it against your cut. It's probably worse than it looks. Head wounds always bleed like a stuck pig.'

Bizarrely, I found myself wondering if he'd ever seen a stuck pig. I did as he suggested wincing until the stinging abated.

'Are you OK to get up?' he asked. 'The others will be getting worried.'

It's surprising what a simple cold compress will do. My shoulder still ached, my head hurt, but the bleeding had stopped and the bump on my skull had receded. I was more concerned about our current predicament.

The water was rising even faster than we had predicted. The shelf on which we had made our original home was already two inches under water. Jag had proven Daniel right by vacating the cavity in the wall he had made his own, and coming to join the rest of us.

It was only a matter of time before we would have to pack up and move on again. Only Daniel and I knew what lay up ahead and how limited were the options that remained, but we had other things on our minds right now. Trouble was brewing.

We had all had something to eat. In my case it was just the packet of crisps. I would have tried to make them last but they were already going soggy so I ate them all. That left just a half a bar of chocolate covered

Kendal mint cake, and a packet of chewing gum.

Jag had nothing left at all. He pleaded with Daniel to let him have something from the stock he'd kept for emergencies.

'Come on Daniel,' he said. 'Just a few peanuts, or some o' them liquorice sweets.'

'No way,' Daniel told him. 'I warned you to take it easy. Why should the rest of us have to suffer because you can't control yourself?'

'But that food's for all of us,' he whined. 'I only want my share.'

'And what happens when that runs out? You'll just come back for more. Anyway, it's for emergencies.'

Jag got to his feet, walked across, and stood over him. 'Who gave you the right to say what an emergency is?'

Daniel jumped to his feet and squared up to him.

'You've been nothing but trouble since we found ourselves in this mess,' he said. 'You think you can do better? Let's put it to the vote.'

They stood there, nose to nose, like a pair of kids in the playground. All it needed was a crowd of Year 7's chanting *Fight! Fight! Fight!* Devon limped over and pushed them apart. It was never going to come to anything. Jag was too much of a coward. He slunk away like a mangy fox with its tail between its legs, and sat down with his back to the rest of us.

'When we've exhausted our supply then you'll get your share,' Daniel called after him. 'Don't worry, there's plenty of water. You're not going to die.'

His voice echoed around the walls and down the tunnels.

You're not going to die...to die...to die...
It was the first time that I had reason to doubt him.

Chapter 16

Peace restored, Daniel sounded the distress signals again. More in hope than expectation. By now it was becoming something of a ritual. Had there been a response it would have taken us all by surprise. We sat back down on our packs to begin to ask our questions of Amina. Nobody seemed to know where to start.

Devon took a deep breath and leaned forward. 'Why doesn't the government in Somalia do something?' he said.

'What government?' Amina replied. 'There is a sort of Federal government but it only has the support of one part of the country. The rest are loyal to groups of warlords, or under the control of the al-Shabaab muhajadeen.'

What about the United Nations?' he persisted.

She smiled sadly. 'Becoming involved in the fighting is out of the question. Who would they choose to side with. Where would they stop? Their major effort is to support over forty thousand refugees flooding into Kenya, and the Yemen, every year. But now the whole of the Middle East is in turmoil. The United Nations is overstretched and running out of money.'

'What about the other African nations?' said Naomi. 'Why don't they get involved?'

'The African Union have been involved for some time,' she replied. 'With the approval of the United Nations. But their role is limited to trying to set up political structures, provide training, and ensure safe passage for humanitarian aid.'

She paused for a drink of water.

'As for getting involved in the fighting, there is no possibility of that. Too many of their countries are either caught up in, or at risk of, civil war. The last thing they would want is to become the target of outside involvement themselves.'

'How many people have died?' said Naomi in that quiet voice of hers.

Amina turned to look directly at her.

'Since 1991, over a million. Some from famine and some from the fighting. They are both connected.'

I sat there trying to take it in. You see it on the television almost every day, either on the news or Red Nose Day, or Sport Relief, and it can start to wash over you, like your brain gets saturated. But when you hear it like this from someone like you, who has lived through it, whose life has been scarred like this, it's impossible not to care. To wonder how you would cope.

'It's alright if you make it to England though in'it?' said Jag, proving me wrong yet again.

'I am not sure what you mean,' she said with a grace that his question did not deserve.

'Like that Somali family in London seekin' asylum like you. Them that live in a pad worth over two million quid. Costin' the taxpayer eight thousand quid a month innit?'

The others turned to glare at him. I didn't want to give him the satisfaction of seeing my anger and upset.

Still Amina was unmoved. Set against all that she had been through his insensitivity must have paled into insignificance.

'I live,' she replied calmly. 'In a terraced house with eight other people. There are three bedrooms. All of the adults have a job. I, and two of my cousins who are also at high school, have part time jobs. Nobody is claiming benefit.'

'How is it that your English is so good?' Naomi asked.

'My father studied English. And he spent a year on a medical exchange in England. He wanted me to be bilingual, so that I would have choices when I grew up.'

Why don't you wear a burqua?' said Devon.

She smiled at him. 'Because it is not a religious requirement - not one of the seven pillars of Islam - nor is it the custom in my father's clan. But I do wear a jihab - a head scarf. Only because it is a custom I have grown accustomed to.'

'Why do you still pray?' he persisted. 'After everything you've been through?'

'You must not confuse religion with faith or Islamism with Islam.'

She reminded me of Mr Roberts, one of our deputy heads, starting one of his morning assembly lectures.

'Neither the cruelty and ignorance of others who profess to share my faith,' she continued. 'Nor the natural disasters that may befall us, are the work of Allah, praise be his name. The harder the challenges that face me, the greater my need for prayer. The more I pray, the deeper my faith becomes.'

It was said with such certainty that it defied contradiction. I think that in the silence that followed we must all have been questioning our personal beliefs. At that moment I coveted a faith as strong as hers. Naomi was the first to recover.

'What kind of things are you not allowed to eat?' She asked.

It fascinated me that Naomi would often want to talk about food and yet she had this obsession to avoid eating it at all costs.

'Just like Daniel we do not eat pork. And we do not eat the meat of any animal that eats another animal.' She smiled. 'But that still leaves many animals that do not. We do not drink alcohol or any kind of intoxicant. And we never eat blood in any form.'

'Who does?' laughed Devon.

'Have you ever eaten black pudding?' she said.

'Of course I have.' His eyes glazed over. 'My grandma used to do a special birthday buffet with black pudding, salt fish, Johnny Cakes, curried pork, stewed mutton, jerk chicken, fish, rice and peas.'

'There you are then,' she said.

Jag looked at Devon 'What's a Johnny cake?' He said.

'It's not Devon's turn,' said Daniel sternly.'

'What do you like most about England Amina?' I asked.

Her eyes widened and her whole face became a huge smile.

'So many things: that it is never too hot or too cold; the rain that makes your hills and fields green; the fact everyone queues in the shops, and for buses and trams. All the things that seem to annoy the English.'

I had never heard her laugh before. It was light and musical like the trill of a song bird.

'Also the National Health Service, and that the streets are clean...'

'That we don't carry guns in the street?' Devon suggested.

Her face clouded over. 'Yes, that too.'

'What don't you like?' said Daniel.

She had to think hard about the answer.

'That you don't seem to appreciate how lucky you are, and how precious your democracy and freedom of speech really is. And that so many people are prepared to live on handouts from the state.'

'Some people don't 'ave a choice,' said Jag.

'Yes they do,' Devon told him bitterly.

I had no idea why Jag's seemingly innocuous comment had touched a nerve with Devon, but all would be revealed in the fullness of time.

'What makes you sad Amina?' said Naomi. 'Apart from the obvious of course.'

The cloud passed over her face again. This time it lingered.

'When I think of the past and of the future I am sad,' she said. 'I remember with happiness and thanksgiving the times that I had with my mother, Al-Hamdu Lillah.' She read the question on our faces and translated. 'All praise and thanks be to Allah. But I am sad when I think of how she died, and that she was not able to see me grow into a woman. I pray for her as a righteous child, and have given to charity on her behalf.'

She reached down for her water and wet her lips.

'As to the future, I worry about my father. He is still in Yemen and there is civil unrest there. I have not heard from him for over a week.' She paused and looked down at the floor. 'And for myself, I worry that I may be deported. My uncle says that if I wish to be certain of remaining here I must agree to a marriage with one of my cousins. He says that my father has sanctioned it.'

'What...like Graeme and Xin in *Coronation Street*?' said Jag, suddenly interested. 'What if the Law finds out?'

She shook her head. 'No, not like that at all. I would have to agree, and I would have the freedom to refuse. It would also be a proper marriage, for life, not pretence until I had my citizenship. You have to understand that it is normal in my culture...my religion. And this would be an arranged marriage, not forced. Such marriages last much longer than your marriages in the West.'

'So it wouldn't be a problem for you?' said Daniel.

She shook her head. 'I did not say that. If I were to marry my cousin I do not think that he would want me to go to University.'

'And you want to?'

She raised her head and although it was probably the reflection from Devon's lamp I thought I detected a determined gleam in her eyes.

'I would like more than anything to be a doctor like my father.'

'Then why,' said Daniel. 'don't you tell your father how you feel?'

Her tone softened and she shook her head slowly.

'Because I do not want to upset him. I can tell that he is still struggling with his grief. Made worse by his feelings of guilt that he was not there to save her.'

'Well I think you should tell 'im,' said Jag. 'He'll understand.'

'Who asked you?' said Daniel, turning on him.

For once I had to agree with Jag.

Chapter 17

The atmosphere had changed for the worse. It was nothing to do with Amina's story. It was a combination of things: the water rising so fast; our having to move from the shelf we had made our home; our scare with Charlie. Jag squaring up to Daniel was just a symptom of how wired we were all getting.

The boredom didn't help. There are only so many times you go to the toilet, or walk to that rock wall Daniel and I had scaled, and back again. Listening to each other's stories did help to take our minds off it but it only worked while they were actually talking, because then you were left with your own thoughts, and the sound of the water lapping the limestone walls.

Even the one minute burst of distress calls were getting on our nerves. Nobody really expected there to be a response anymore. I could tell by the way they carried on with what they were doing and didn't even bother to listen. That clouded the exercise with an overwhelming sense of futility. Not that we didn't expect to be rescued. At that stage I think we all believed that it would happen. It was just that there didn't seem to be anything that we could do to hurry it along. We were powerless.

Daniel's insistence that we follow the clock, and keep to day and night with meal times as they would have been above the ground, did help. Not that there was anything much to eat anymore. I only found out afterwards that having a routine was the most important part of keeping us sane. I still don't know if Daniel had been aware of that – maybe from following the Chilean miners' story – or if he just knew instinctively that it was right. I'll have to remember to ask him.

Getting to sleep was becoming increasingly difficult. At first I think we'd been living on adrenalin, and when that leached out it left you exhausted. But as we became accustomed to our situation that was no longer the case. With so little to do and hardly any exercise I wasn't really tired when it came to lights out. I say lights out, but there was still that faint glow from Devon's lamp that Daniel had now worked out how to hood with a helmet. I know it was really there to help Charlie with his fear of darkness, but I was secretly glad of it too.

That night I prayed myself to sleep. It wasn't something I had done since I was child, but I had never had as good a reason, or needed more the comfort that it seemed to bring. I prayed, in turn, for each of my companions trapped in the cave. Then I prayed for my parents, that God would let them know that I was still alive and safe. I prayed for my sister Beth. That she was in Heaven, looking down on me right now. That she would help to keep me safe, even though I had failed to manage that for her.

Finally, I prayed for myself. There was a prayer my mother taught me that I used to say as a child last thing at night.

Angel of God my Guardian dear, to whom God's love

commits me here, ever this night be at my side, to light, to guard, to rule, and guide.

I'm not sure that I believe in angels, let alone in one specially reserved for me. But you have no idea how simply repeating that little rhyme took me back twelve years to my lovely warm bed, in my cosy little bedroom with the mobiles overhead, and my teddy bear in the crook of my arm, tucked up safe underneath the covers.

Wednesday 1st of June

When I woke it was cold and damp. The whole of my right side was stiff from contact with the limestone floor. I shifted painfully onto my left side and tried to ignore the pins and needles as blood coursed back into my arm and leg.

'Grace, are you awake?'

I opened my eyes. Amina stared straight back at me. It was unnerving how close she was.

'Just about,' I whispered back.

She smiled, and stretched luxuriously, like a contented cat.

'I have been lying here listening to the sound of the water,' she said. 'Watching it shimmer in the reflected light. It is almost magical.'

I lay back and turned my head towards the sound of water bubbling up gently from the centre, sending concentric waves in silver ripples across the surface. Amina was right. Under any other circumstances this would have been a moment to savour.

I turned back to face her. 'You must really miss your mother.'

She smiled and nodded. 'I will always miss her. Her smile, her wisdom, her love, her laugh.'

'You've got her smile and her laugh I think,' I said.

Her face lit up. 'You are right, or so everyone tells me. And I know it from the expression on my father's face when he sees me smile, or hears me laugh. He is happy and sad, both at the same time.'

'A bitter sweet memory.'

'It must be like that for you...with Beth I mean,' she whispered gently.

'It is,' I told her. 'More sweet than bitter as time has gone on. But sometimes I'll see someone who looks a little like her – like the person she would be now if she had lived – and it's like someone has stabbed me in the heart with a tiny needle.'

'I know what you mean,' she said. 'Only for me the hurt is still raw and the stab is like a dagger.'

I had no reply to that. We lay there in silence listening to the sound of water lapping the sides of the cavern, and dripping from the rock formations, and the cross rhythmic breathing of our companions. It was a long way from the Fingal's Cave overture by Mendelssohn that I performed at the Bridgewater Hall with the Manchester Schools Orchestra last year, but every bit as haunting. I know which of the two I shall carry with me to my grave.

Breakfast that morning was a sombre affair. We'd finally caught up with Jag. None of us had any food left at all. No, that's not strictly true. Naomi still had half of a muesli bar left, but apart from that there was just the emergency stash from Matt's pack that Daniel had been guarding.

'Right,' he said, laying them down one by one. 'There are two packets of chocolate covered peanuts, a 200 gram bag of Pontefract cakes, and one self heating Lancashire hot pot.'

'How are we going to share them out?' said Devon.

'I suggest we count out the Pontefract cakes and divide by six.' he replied. 'Then divide each packet of peanuts between three of us.'

'What about the hot pot?' said Jag, who hadn't eaten anything for over twenty four hours. 'Naomi's a veggie, and the lamb's gotta be kosher, so that's you and Amina out innit?'

'Lamb *is* kosher,' Daniel told him.

'Not if ain't killed right,' Jag retorted.

'We don't how it was killed,' said Daniel. 'And anyway I think you're confusing me with a religious zealot. You obviously haven't been listening have you?'

'It is alright Daniel,' said Amina. ' Let him have my share. It is not worth fighting over.'

'She's right,' said Devon. 'There'll only be a spoonful each as it is.

'Can I give you all some advice?' said Naomi as we contemplated our tiny piles of liquorice and chocolate covered peanuts. 'Before you eat anything drink a whole bottle of water. Then you won't feel as hungry, and you won't be tempted to eat too many at once.'

It dawned on me that this was something Naomi had been doing all along. And not just here in the cave. Back at school she always seemed to have a bottle of mineral water in her hand.

'It's called water loading,' she said. 'Something I learned on the inside.'

It turned out that she was right. It's surprising how such a small thing can make such a difference, especially when you see the days and nights stretching bleakly ahead of you like a road to nowhere. And time is running out.

Chapter 18
Naomi's Story

'I know what everyone thinks,' she said. 'That I'm some kind of freak who chooses to look like this because that's what models look like.'

She could see that I was about to protest and held her hand palm up to stop me.

'OK, maybe not everyone but *most* people. To be fair, I don't get the same kind of cat calling and vile texts I got back home. Just the looks. Anyway, my point is this is not a life choice, it's a disease. That's why my parents sent me to the St Jude's Abbey Centre.'

She shook her head as though she couldn't believe it had really happened.

'Like an idiot I thought they called it that because it was like some kind of retreat house with ivy climbing over gothic arches. Maybe with a wishing well in the grounds. You know the kind of thing. It was only after I'd been there a week or so I found out that ABBEY stood for Anorexic, Bulimic, Binge Eating Youth, and that St Jude was the patron of lost or hopeless causes. Somebody's sick idea of a joke I guess. Well the joke was on me. But I tell you something, I learned plenty in that place. How to fake and hide and sham, how to fool myself and everyone else except for my fellow sufferers who'd taught me all the tricks in the first place. Not necessarily what they hoped I would learn, but plenty all the same.

It turned out to be a brand new building – all wood, and glass and steel – in the grounds of a former monastery in the Catskills. It was Tuesday when I got there, just in time for a weighing session. Three times a week - first thing in the morning – they made us change out of our pyjamas into a thin cotton shift before getting on the weigh scales. I began to dread it. Because I'm anorexic I was terrified I might have gained weight, but if I hadn't put any on the staff would make me feel guilty and redouble their efforts to get me to eat. That's what I call a no win situation.

I would wake up early on weigh days, sometimes as early as half past three, and lay there trying to work out how much I'd eaten over the past two days, how much extra exercise I'd put in when nobody was watching. Early on I learned from the other girls that if you drank a load of water before they weighed you it would look like you'd put on weight when you hadn't. But pretty soon the staff got wise to the fact I was doing that and made me go for a pee before I went down to the weighing room.

Those weighing sessions were the start of a routine that was so oppressive it felt like I was in prison. After we'd been weighed there was medication and again last thing at night. We had six meals a day. Breakfast was at seven am, then a mid morning snack at ten, followed by lunch at twelve thirty. Tea was at three thirty, dinner at seven, and supper at nine. We sat six to a table. Each table had a nurse or senior carer who watched our every move. And believe me, they had to. We were up to every trick in the trade.'

She smiled at the thought of it.

'Bread and biscuits and fruit you'd hide up your sleeves or down the front of your pants. Some girls would chew their food until it was like a paste and then stick it to the underside of the table. It was like the surface of the moon under there. We even had competitions to see who could get away with hiding the most food. One day I was searched on the way out of the refectory and it was like they'd caught a shoplifter in the mall. You could have fed an army on what I had down the front of my sweater.

I got hauled before the matron and she declared me UC - an Uncooperative. That meant they put me on a regime of Cognitive Behavioural Therapy - CBT to you and me. In reality the whole of our time there was a sort of CBT, but I got individual sessions as well as the group therapy we had every day. The group stuff was a waste of time because everybody was simply playing the game. We were supposed to be completely honest with each other but the reality was that we only told the real truth when we were on our own. That's when we taught each other the tricks we used to avoid eating food or putting on weight, and swapped stories about the staff.'

She took the top off her bottle and had a drink. She smiled as she screwed the top back on again

'I know what you're thinking but that wasn't water loading, my mouth was really dry from all this talking.'

I thought it was great that she could make jokes about her condition like that.

'The staff, they were something else,' she continued. 'We used to call the Director the Governor, and the Matron the Senior Warder. The nurses and care assistants who sat on our tables at meal times we christened the Calorie Cops. When we saw one of the staff coming someone would call out *Five Oh!* or *Six Up!* There are cops approaching, or there are cops behind you. They even watched us to make sure we used the lift to get to the dormitory so we wouldn't try to burn up the calories by climbing the stairs.'

She sensed our disbelief and looked around the circle slowly so that we could see that she was serious.

'I'm not joking. We even had to go and lie down for an hour after every meal so we would digest the food properly. The toilets were out of bounds so the bulimics among us couldn't bring it all up. We used to try and get our own back by standing up when we should be sitting down, and walking back and forth along the corridors when we were chatting. We found any way we could to burn off those calories.

In my case – little Miss Uncooperative – they took away all my privileges and made me earn them back, one at a time. If I wanted a book or a magazine to read I had to gain two pounds in weight. My iPod cost me four pounds. A bath or shower one pound eight ounces, and a phone call two and a half pounds.'

Let me tell you it, was just like I imagine prison must be. There was one girl there who'd been in Juvenile Hall upstate who said it was even worse than prison. It created an *us against them* mentality, and just like prison makes you a better criminal – one who learns how to avoid getting caught next time – so we learned how to hide our eating disorders better on the outside.'

She looked down at the ground for a moment. It was a sign that I was beginning to recognise in every one who had told a story so far, myself included. She was remembering something powerful; a painful memory that required her to keep her emotions under control.

'All the time I was in that place it was like I was in suspended animation. The one thing that is left to an anorexic – to anyone with any kind of eating disorder – is the power to decide what to eat, when to eat, and when not to. It's the only part of our lives that we can control. And when they took that away I was left with nothing.'

'The bastards,' muttered Devon.

'Not really,' she said surprising us all. 'There was method in their madness. It may have been hell but at least I discovered that I could put on weight and it wouldn't kill me. If anything I now have more control than I did when I went in there. I may not have the body image my parents want for me, or the weight that doctors tell me is healthy, but I'm more at ease with myself.'

'Can I ask a question now?' said Devon.

She picked up her water bottle. 'Sure.'

'You mentioned *back home*; where is that exactly, and who was it that cat-called you and sent those text messages.?'

'That's two questions,' said Jag.

Devon made a rude gesture in his direction.

Her face lit up. 'Back home is Binghamton, the capital of Broome County. It's a small city to the North West of New York, near the border with Pennsylvania. It's in a valley where two rivers meet; the Susquehanna and the Chenango. It's real pretty.'

'What's the weather like?' asked Daniel.

'The summers are warm and wet – a bit like here - except the temperatures back home are regularly in the 80s Fahrenheit, and can reach as high as the 90's. But the winters are real cold and we get lots of snow; at least six foot most years and it can drift up to twice that height, no problem.'

'The text messages?' Devon reminded her.

'Some of that was at high school,' she said. 'But mostly it was at summer camp in my seventh grade year at junior high. My parents only sent me the once. They said it would be character building. My character it nearly destroyed. It was so bad I ran away and hitchhiked all the way back home.' She grinned. 'Eight hundred and fifty miles. My Mom was almost out of her mind when I turned up on our porch out of the blue.'

Why did you come to England, Naomi?' I asked.

'My dad is on an exchange programme at British Aerospace as part of the US/UK co-operation on space exploration, and my mom is teaching at the University here,' she said. 'But I think they really arranged all that in the hope that it would help my condition if they brought me to England.'

'How come they thought that?' said Daniel.

'Well back home I was surrounded by people who either shovelled up their food in the belief that big is beautiful, or ones like me who went in the other direction. I guess they thought I would be exposed to a lot more 'normal' role models over here in the UK.'

'And were you?'

'You tell me,' she replied. 'You only have to walk down Market Street or go into the Food Hall in the Trafford Centre on a Saturday, and it looks to me like you're racing to catch us up.'

'Why do you think you do it?' said Jag. 'You know, the anorexia thing?'

She didn't let it phase her. Instead she smiled and patiently replied. 'Like I said earlier Jag, it's not really a choice, although I used to kid myself it was. It's a compulsion born out of a disease; a disorder if you like, like depression. I never asked for it and I sure as hell wish I was rid of it. That's as near an answer as I can give you, or myself.'

I was uncomfortable with the way the questions always seemed to come back to Naomi's anorexia. As though it was the only thing about her; as though it defined her.

'What do you like about England?' I said. 'And is there anything that's disappointed you?'

'Good question,' she said, as she unscrewed the top of her bottle and took another sip. 'I love your pop music. We have Country, Hip Hop, R&B, Freak Folk, and even Christian punk and Christian rap, but yours is so much more diverse, and thoughtful I think. What else? Oh yeh, I love your TV programmes, and all the historical sites, and that the distances are so much shorter between places. I like that people are more tolerant and patient with strangers than in New York, that your streets are cleaner and, above all, that the portions you serve in restaurants and cafes means that it's much harder to put on weight!'

There it was again; her capacity to laugh at herself. Maybe it was living over here. Maybe we'd helped her to figure out irony?

'What don't you like?' said Daniel.

'It's so damn expensive,' she said grimacing. 'Like your restaurants are twice as much – not that that really bothers me - and the gas for your tank is three times the price back home. And that's another thing;

I could drive at fifteen with a permit back home. Over here you can't drive till you're seventeen, and the insurance is way too prohibitive. What else? You don't put enough ice in your cokes, and you're always going on about the weather.'

I thought she had pegged us pretty well.

'What is that makes you happy, and what is that makes you sad Naomi?' Amina asked.

'It pisses me off, *and* makes me sad, the way we treat our planet. Burning down the forests, poisoning the seas, the way they slaughter the whales and the seals, and trap the dolphins.'

She was more animated than I had ever seen her. Waving her stick thin arms and shaking her head.

'While millions of people are dying all over the world from lack of basic necessities like water, and grain, and medicine, the rich nations are stockpiling food to keep up the price, paying slave wages to children in sweat factories, and charging prices for essential drugs that they'll never be able to afford. It makes me mad!'

Jag stared at her in amazement. The rest of us had instinctively leaned back, buffeted by the ferocity of her words. It wasn't what she had said, rather the passion and violence with which she had said it. She took several deep breaths, and then reached for her water bottle.

'It is a shame more people do not feel these things as strongly as you Naomi,' said Amina. 'Especially those in government, and those who run the big corporations. The world would be a much better and fairer place.'

'Amen to that,' said Daniel.

'So what makes you happy?' asked Devon in a tone that suggested that he doubted if anything could pull off that particular miracle.

She put the bottle down, and looked slowly around the circle of faces.

'Being here with you.'

Her words hung in the air like a lost chord. I couldn't decide if that was the saddest or most comforting thing that I had ever heard.

Chapter 19

That afternoon something happened to raise our hopes. Charlie and Devon had gone to the loo together – there was no way after what happened yesterday that we were going to let Charlie go unaccompanied – when Charlie came rushing back on his own.

'Come quick,' he said breathlessly. 'We heard something. There's someone down here. Devon said for Daniel to bring his whistle.'

The six of us stood on either side of the sump hole, staring down into the depths; straining to hear the slightest sound out of the ordinary. Daniel and Devon were on their knees hoping that extra metre would give them an advantage. All I could hear was the sound of rushing water.

'There,' said Devon his voice tight with excitement. 'That's it.'

I heard a faint clinking sound, as though something metallic had banged against a piece of rock.

'Blow the whistle!' he shouted.

Daniel kept it on a lanyard clipped to his belt so he could find it in a hurry. The cord had become entangled and he struggled to free it.

'Hurry up!' Jag urged.

Daniel yanked it loose and put it to his lips. Three shrill blasts filled the narrow space. The tension was almost unbearable as we waited for the echoes to fade.

'Try again,' said Naomi.

As Daniel raised the whistle to his lips three faint blasts rose up from the depths below us. My heart leapt in my chest, and hot blood sped through my veins.

'There's someone there!' Jag shouted

Amina grasped my arm and hung on tight, as though – like me - she could barely believe what was happening.

'Do it again,' said Devon.

This time the response to Daniel's signal was longer in coming. No more than a couple of seconds, but it seemed like an age.

Immediately he sounded another three blasts. Now the interval was even longer. Jag began to yell into that hole.

'Help! Help! We're here! Help us!'

Everyone joined in. We shouted until our voices were hoarse. Daniel stood up and waved his arms to quieten us down.

"We've got to give them a chance to respond.' he said. 'Let's listen for a minute.'

We heard nothing but the onward rush of the underground river.

'Try again with the whistle,' said Devon. 'Maybe they're too busy making their way towards us to stop and shout back.'

This time there was no response at all.

Devon used his good leg to stand up, one hand against the tunnel wall for extra support.

'All the twists and turns and caverns, and false tunnels down here,' he said. 'Must make it difficult to know where sounds are coming from. At least they know that we're still alive. They'll keep looking till they find us.'

I could tell from the way their shoulders had drooped, and the fact that none of us could look each other in the eyes, that nothing was going to reassure us now. The disappointment was still too raw. Suddenly I realised that Charlie was no longer with us.

'Where's Charlie?!' I shouted.

In a panic I pushed past the others and started down the tunnel. As I reached the first bend I saw the light from his helmet. I found him, huddled against the wall, cradling his knees to his chest. I sat down beside him and placed my hand on his shoulder.

'What's the matter Charlie?'

'I knew they wouldn't find us,' he said.

It was the way he said it that worried me most. There was no hint of self pity, sadness, or despair, just a flat, calm, certainty.

'They're never going to find us.'

I slid my arm around his shoulders and hugged him tight.

'Of course they will,' I told him. 'At least now they know we are here. They're going to move heaven and earth to get us out. It's only a matter of time. We just need to be patient.'

I'd done a good job of persuading myself, but Charlie was not convinced. As he turned his face towards mine I saw the resignation in his eyes.

'They won't come Grace,' he said. 'They never come.'

The remainder of the day was shrouded in silent despondency. None of us could think of anything to say. Daniel paced up and down, the rest of us sat alone, wrapped up in our own thoughts. If mine were anything to go by they were melancholy imaginings.

I wondered how my parents would be right now. My mother would already have made up her mind that I was dead. She would be inconsolable. Bad enough to have lost one daughter, but to have lost two would be unbearable. My father, wrapped up in his own grief, would be finding it impossible to comfort her, much as he knew he needed to. At church the entire congregation would be praying for me; showering my parents with tea and cakes and sympathy, and words of hope eternal.

At school my friends would be in a state of shock. Melanie would be staying positive, telling the others it was going to be alright. Rianna would be writing my eulogy, and Helen suggesting songs for the memorial service. I knew that the others would be thinking much the same. Except for Naomi, who had probably been through this exercise several times already, and Charlie of course. I wondered if there was anyone who would really miss Charlie, apart from us.

'Shit! My lamp's buggered,' whined Jag

'Serves you right for leaving it on too long,' said Daniel.

'Mine's on its last legs by the looks of it.' Devon – pointed to the wan glow from the alcove where Daniel had placed it when Matt's had failed.

'That's it then,' said Daniel in that commanding tone he had now perfected. 'No other lamps on apart from this one, unless you're going to the loo. And even then only one lamp between you.'

'That means we have to rely on a girl to go with us,' Jag complained.

'You don't need to worry, we'll turn our backs.' Naomi told him. 'Nobody wants to watch you having a wee.'

I won't repeat what he said, but it caused Devon to throw a handful of loose stones in his direction, sending him scuttling into the shadows.

'Look we can't just sit here moping about,' said Daniel. 'It just makes it worse. Come on Devon it's your turn. See if you can't cheer us up.'

Judging by the first three stories, Daniel's, Amina's and mine, I doubted it. But you just never know.

Chapter 20
Devon's Story

'In case you haven't noticed,' he began. 'My ankle's getting better. Thanks to Grace. It's not a hundred percent, but it's getting there. I'm telling you this because I reckon that's true of most things. They're never as bleak as they seem at first. They almost always get better in the end. And that's what my story is about.

My father named me after Devon Malcolm, a famous West Indies fast bowler.'

He grinned, and his teeth shone brightly even in the muted glow of the failing lamp.

'It could have been worse. He could have chosen Viv, after Viv Richards.'

He searched for his water bottle in the pack beside him, held it up, realised that it was empty, and set it down.

'My father was a bastard.'

He made it sound matter of fact.

'The only favour he did her was that they never got married. So I guess that makes me a bastard too. He gave her two sons - Jerome is four years older than me - three miscarriages, and more beatings than I care to remember.'

Amina reached out, took his water bottle, and made her way to the water's edge where she proceeded to fill it.

'We never knew when he was going to be home. He had three other women on the go that I know of, probably more. But our house was the bolt hole he came back to most of the time.'

'We were all scared of him. It was him that got my mother into serious drinking. First off as his boozing partner, and then to dull the pain and fear that came with having him as her partner. It wasn't till I went to school that I realised that ours wasn't a normal household. The very first sleep over I was invited to was a revelation. It was like entering another world; one where the adults were nice to each other. Where they weren't shouting, screaming and fighting, lying in bed all day, or sprawled out on the sofa three sheets to the wind.'

Amina handed him the bottle.

'Thanks Mina,' he said taking a long hard swig. He screwed the top on slowly and deliberately and placed in on the ground beside him.

'I was ten years old when Mum said we were moving. It was late at night after the worst of their fights. She gave us a rucksack each to put all of our stuff in, filled a suitcase with what few belongings she had, and then we set off. It was all of a mile and a half, to a women's' refuge near the old Man City Stadium on Maine Road. Three months we were there. My father started hanging around outside school trying to get us to tell where we were staying. When we wouldn't he tried to bribe us with skunk, then money, and finally he started threatening what he'd do to us. When all that failed he started trying to follow us. That was when Jerome did his thing.'

He placed his hands on the floor, on either side of his body, and leaned back on them to relieve the pressure on his backside.

'Jerome was already connected by then. He'd been acting as a runner for one of the two drugs gangs on our estate. I knew, mainly because he was always buying the latest trainers and tops, and he was always flush with money. Our mum was too busy with her own problems to notice. Either that, or she didn't care.

Anyway, he got the loan of a gun. I thought it was a replica but it was a proper one. A converted Russian Baikal gas pistol. It had three bullets in it. He put it in his kit bag and took it to school, but he didn't show it to anyone. Sure enough when we came out of school our father was doing a bad job of trying to hide behind a swanky four by four. Jerome said to let him follow us. We headed off towards Alexandra Park.

Jerome waited till we passed a large rhododendron bush, then pulled me off the path and made me crouch behind him. Our father walked past. He stopped because he couldn't work out where we'd gone. Jerome stood up with the gun held steady in his hand.

"Hello bastard," he said. "Where the fuck d'you think you're going?"

I don't know which of the two of us was the most frightened; me or my father. I thought he was going to call Jerome's bluff. Grab the pistol off him and give us the beating of our lives. But he didn't. He just stood there shaking; his face white, and sort of caved in.

"There's no need for this," he said, his voice trembling. "I just wanted to see your mum. To tell her I'm sorry...to make it all right, for her...for you two."

Jerome let him babble on until he ran out of words. He could see he was wetting his pants and was enjoying every moment of it.

"I'll tell you how you can make it all right," he said. "You can piss off out of her life, and ours, and don't come back...ever."

"But I love her..." he began.

Jerome cut him off with a wave of his gun. "You never loved her you bastard, you just used her. Anyway it's not up for discussion. I'm going to count to ten, and if you're not out of my sight by then I'm going to come after you and kill you. And if you ever come sniffing around her again I'll kill you. And if you try to get even with me, the mates that got me this gun will pick you up off the street one night and you'll never be seen again. Except maybe in little pieces here and there."

He steadied the gun and pointed it straight at where our father's heart would have been, if he'd actually had one, and began to count.

"One...two...three...four..."

It took that long for our father to decide if Jerome was serious and, if he was, whether or not he had the balls to pull that trigger. Then he was gone. Running like the wind. Jerome continued to count.

"Five...six...seven...eight...nine..."

On the count of ten he extended his arm, clicked his tongue, raised the pistol, and blew gently across the hole from which the bullets would have sped.

"Goodbye bastard," he said.

He put the gun back in his kit bag, then turned to me and pulled me to my feet. It was only then that I realised that I was the one who'd wet my pants. Jerome laughed. "Come on Junior," he said. "Don't

worry you'll have dried out before we get to the road."
Then he set off whistling the tune to *The First of the
Gang to Die*, by Morrissey.'

He smiled and flashed those teeth again.

'I didn't even know he was a fan of Morrissey.'

He paused for a moment to rub his ankle, and
shifted his position to get comfortable.

'Our father never bothered us again after that. The
council re-housed us, and the woman at the hostel
arranged for an injunction against him coming
anywhere near us. I see him from time to time going
in or coming out of pubs. We never speak.'

He had another drink of water. Normally when
we did that it was for a reason: because our throats
had dried up; because we'd become too emotional; for
dramatic effect. In Devon's case I had no idea which
it was other than it formed a natural break, like the
start of a new chapter.

'Jerome got deeper into the gang,' he continued.
'He left home when he was seventeen. Now he's
twenty two, and living with his girl friend. The mate
he got the gun off turned out to be our cousin Kyle.
He died two years ago in a drive by shooting. As
more and more of the gang got shot, or put inside,
Jerome moved on up the pecking order. He's cock of
the walk now, in every sense. The way he's going he
may not be the first of the gang to die, but he's
probably going to be the next one.'

For the first time I thought I detected some emotion
in his voice.

'Are you in a gang?' Jag asked with his customary
tact.

Devon regarded him with something approaching contempt.

'No I'm not in a gang. I never will be. Why would I? It's pathetic, and cowardly and self-destructive. And I've been lucky. Shortly after Kyle was killed my mother got a visit from the police and an Education Welfare Officer. She assumed the worst - that Jerome had been killed in a revenge attack – and lost it. It took two of them, and me, to stop her harming herself. It turned out they were there to talk about me. They were worried that I would get sucked into Jerome's gang and end up just like Kyle. They were from something called MMAGS – the Manchester Multi Agency Gangs Strategy- trying to prevent the siblings of gang members from going the same way.'

He had another drink and wiped his mouth with the back of his hand. It was the first time I really registered how large his hands were, like dinner plates. I thought he would have made a great goalkeeper.

'They got me enrolled in the Amaechi Basketball Centre. That's when I found out I could really play the game. I worked my way up to first team juniors. I've made a load of mates.' He smiled contentedly. 'I don't need a gun in my hand to make me feel special, just a basketball.'

'Do you believe in God?' said Naomi.

Devon looked at her full on for a moment. It was almost as though he was trying to guess what she hoped he would say.

'No,' he said. 'I don't. My mother does, and it's never done her any good, and my father thought he was God and look where that got him. I've not had the best of examples to follow when it comes to religion.'

'Where do you think you'll go when you die then?' She said.

I guess it was a question we'd all been wrestling with in the dark of the night, ever since the tunnel had collapsed. It still came as a shock to hear it said out loud. Like a challenge that could no longer be avoided.

'I don't know,' he said. 'But I don't suppose it will matter very much either way. If there's no afterlife I'll never know. If there is, it'll come as a nice surprise.'

'So long as you stick to basketball,' said Daniel.

Our nervous laughter echoed around the walls of the cave.

'If I'm honest,' said Devon. 'There have been times when I was more scared of living than dying.'

'I know what you mean,' said Naomi.

Beside her, Charlie's head drooped even further and I could have sworn that he had started to cry.

Amina's voice came softly out of the shadows. 'But you are both still here, and I am very thankful.'

Chapter 21

Thursday 2nd June

That night it proved almost impossible to sleep. What sleep I did get was fitful. In the intervals in between I alternated between feeling nauseous and so tired that I promised God that I would do anything – become a nun and dedicate my life to prayer, give everything I had to the poor - whatever it would take to get an hour of uninterrupted slumber. Looking back I realise that I had made no such promises to get us out of there. I suppose it goes to prove why sleep deprivation is such an effective form of torture.

Morning brought the mother of all headaches. Hunger gnawed at my insides like a rat. I only knew that it was morning because Daniel told me so.

'Wake up Grace,' he said, shaking me gently. A hammer bounced from one side of my skull to the other. 'The water's rising. We have to move again.'

I rubbed the sleep from my eyes, sat up, and looked around. It was as though someone had suddenly turned a tap on full. The water was cascading over the rim of our shelf and within ten minutes would be lapping our boots. Even the sound of our voices had changed now that so much of the space had been inundated. The others were already scrambling to put their pitiful possessions in their packs.

'Whatever caused that tunnel to collapse must have diverted an underground stream,' Devon called over. 'Daniel says maybe it moved some kind of plug that's caused a lake on a higher level to drain down here.'

I put my arms through the straps of my pack and shrugged it on. For the first time since we'd moved onto the shelf I felt an almost uncontainable fear. From the outset I had convinced myself that it was only a matter of time before we were found. The response to our alarm calls by the swallow hole above Leck Beck had reinforced that conviction. Now I could imagine the water rushing through the tunnel down which we were about to flee, pouring into the sump as it must have done centuries before, drowning those who sought to save us, cutting off our only means of escape. I didn't know which would be worse, drowning or starving to death. My legs had turned to jelly.

'Bring everything,' said Daniel. 'Bottles, empty wrappers, the lot. You never know what we might need.' He turned to me. 'Are you OK to bring the rope ladder Grace? I've got an extra lamp to carry, Devon's ankle is still dodgy, Amina's keeping an eye on Charlie, and...'

'It's fine,' I told him. 'It was my idea to hang onto it. I agreed to carry it.'

He grinned. Shadows in the hollows beneath his eyes and cheekbones gave his face a ghoulish appearance. 'I think you'll find I didn't give you a choice.'

'I always had a choice,' I snapped back at him. 'I could have just left it there.'

He held up his hands in submission. 'Whoa,' he said. 'It was only a joke.'

I bent down, picked up the ladder, and hoisted it over my left shoulder. He held out his hand.

'Here let me.'

Without a word I brushed passed him and followed the others into the tunnel. I was ashamed of myself. Daniel's style of leadership had begun to grate on us all but I knew it was petty of me to overreact like that. Nobody else had been prepared to take it on. Without him I hate to think how it might have turned out down there.

We trudged wordlessly down the tunnels pausing by the sump hole while Daniel tried once more with the whistle. When the last of the echoes had faded, behind the sounds of the stream far below, silence mocked us.

'It's bloody steep!'

It was the only time I recall Devon having sworn which, given everything he'd been through, came as a real surprise. Along with the others he stared up at the sheer wall of the rock pile.

'Don't worry,' Daniel told him. 'It's a piece of cake, even with your ankle. Grace and I managed it no problem, didn't we Grace?'

Tactfully put. I realised that he was trying to make amends.

'That's right Daniel,' I said. 'No problem.'

'Once we get over this it's plain sailing all the way to the ravine,' he said. 'There's bound to be a way out somewhere, we didn't have time to look properly did we Grace?'

'No Daniel,' I replied, the lie sticking in my throat.

Daniel climbed up first with Matt's rope over one

shoulder and the rope ladder over the other. Naomi and I shone our lamps from either side to light his way. Once on top he positioned himself on the choke stone, then set up the rope with the descenders and lowered it over the far side for the descent. Then he secured the rope ladder as best he could as an aid for the rest of us to use on the final stages of our climb up to join him. As the only one left who had already scaled that wall I went last.

Jag scaled it first with surprising agility and far more courage than he had shown on the Go Ape course. That seemed an age ago now; a dim and distant memory from another existence. Charlie managed it, his tentative progress encouraged by Amina who followed close behind him guiding his every move.

Naomi found it far more difficult; the weakness of her famished frame cruelly exposed by the steepness of the climb and the strength and endurance required by those holds at the extremity of her reach. Had it not been for Devon, all thoughts of the pain in his ankle set aside, climbing beside her and helping with advice and a judicious heave from time to time, she would have fallen several times.

By the time I reached the safety of the choke stone Jag, Charlie and Amina had already arrived at the bottom on the other side, and Devon and Naomi were half way down. This time Devon was leading. I could tell that the pain had finally got through the initial rush of adrenaline by the grunts each time his weight came down on that foot.

'I don't know about you,' said Daniel as we lay side by side watching their painful progress. 'But I never thought they'd all make it.'

'A piece of cake?' I whispered.

'What else was I supposed to say?'

That grin again. It seemed to be reserved for me alone. We had become confidants and co-conspirators, in a conspiracy to hide the inevitable for as long as possible.

'There's bound to be a way out?' I said.

He put his lips close to my ear. 'Maintenance of hope Grace. The maintenance of hope.'

'It's amazing!' exclaimed Devon.

It was exactly the feeling I had experienced the first time I set eyes on this place. We stood in a line at the end of the passage staring into the chamber with its sand coloured floor, ribbed walls banded with orange and amethyst, vaulted ceiling, and the dark pool at its furthest margin. It struck me as smaller now that I was seeing it for the second time, but no less beautiful.

'Harah!' Said Daniel striking his forehead with the heel of his hands. 'Nim'as li!' He saw us staring at him. 'I left Matt's rucksack on the other side of the wall. The rest of you go ahead and settle yourselves down in there. I won't be long.'

'Do you want me to hold the rope?' I asked.

He shook his head. The light from his lamp formed crazy patterns on the roof of the tunnel. 'It's alright Grace. I can manage,' he said.

Jag made a beeline for the largest cleft in the right hand wall, threw his pack on the floor, and snuggled in. He started talking to himself and anyone else who cared to listen.

'So much for Mr Clever Dick. *'I forgot Matt's pack!'* He'd forget his head if it wasn't screwed on. The big man... self-appointed leader. He couldn't lead his way out of the Trafford Centre!'

'What's that, your best sargasm?' Said Devon. 'Shut it Jag, before I come and shut it for you.'

'Oh yeah?' Jag replied, giving him the finger. 'You an' whose army?'

Before Devon could respond Jag was overcome by a fit of coughing. It went on so long that I was worried that he was choking. His chest heaved with the strain. In between bouts he fought for his breath. Amina and I arrived by his side together. By now he was doubled over. Amina took hold of his shoulders from the front. I began to pat him hard on the back. That only seemed to make it worse. Instinctively I encircled his body with both arms and held on tight trapping the convulsions in his chest.

Slowly, miraculously, the spasms died down until we were able to lay him on the floor of the cave. He curled up in the foetus position, each breath-in a gulp, each breath-out a sigh. Amina took the water bottle from his pack and found it was empty. She went to get hers, unscrewed the top, and handed it to him.

'Here Jag, drink this,' she said.

He drank slowly, cautiously, as though he expected the coughing to erupt at any moment. Despite the bright light of our lamps I could tell that his face had gone pale. He looked frightened and small, as though he had shrunk into himself. More like Charlie than the Jag we had come to know.

'You shouldn't get so excited,' Devon called over.

'Leave him be,' said Naomi. 'Can't you see he's sick?'

'*Sick* is how he's been since the minute that tunnel caved in,' Devon replied. 'This is a welcome relief.

This should be his normal.'

A cry, accompanied by the sound of rocks falling, echoed through the chamber cutting off Naomi's reply.

'Oh my God! That's Daniel,' she cried, jumping to her feet and running into the passage that led back to the rock fall. I left Amina by Jag's side and hurried after her, my heart as cold as ice.

Daniel lay at the foot of the wall on his left side. Naomi knelt beside him. He was clutching his right arm as though in pain.

'I thought we might need the rope,' he said. 'So I untied it at the top, and started down with it over my shoulder. My foot slipped, and I fell. I landed on my arm. I think I've broken it.'

'Do you think you can stand?' I asked.

'It's my arm not my leg,' he groaned. 'I'll give it a try.'

I hooked my left hand gingerly beneath his arm pit. Naomi did same on his good side. He leant on her as we pulled him gently to his feet. As we started to move towards the tunnel he winced with pain.

'I'm sorry,' I said.

'It's me that should be sorry,' he replied. 'After all this I couldn't find that damn rucksack. The water's already two feet up the far side.' He stopped to make sure he had our attention. 'Listen, for God's sake don't tell the others. Jag and Charlie will only panic.'

Charlie's already given up,' Naomi told him. 'And I think you'll find Jag has other things on his mind.'

She was right. Devon and Naomi came over to see how he was and share their concern but Jag was curled up in a ball, too consumed with self-pity to give a damn about Daniel's misfortune.

'What was that you said back there?' I asked him when the others had gone to explore. 'Just before you went back for the pack.' He smiled weakly. I don't think he had the strength to grin.

'It means, Shit! I've had enough,' he said. 'But don't tell the others or that's my authority stuffed, if it isn't already.'

'How's your arm feeling now?'

He tested it cautiously. 'It still hurts like hell but I don't think it is broken. Maybe it's just badly bruised.'

'Can I feel it?' I said. 'I promise I'll be careful.'

'You don't have to promise Grace,' he replied. 'You I trust.'

I ran my hand gently down each side of his upper arm in turn.

'At least there's nothing protruding,' I told him. 'Can you move your fingers?'

'No problem,' He said curling and uncurling them to prove it. 'The pain's higher up. At the top of my arm.'

I slid my hands up his arm and began probing with my fingertips.

'Ow!' he yelled, flinching as I hurriedly released my grip.

'I'm sorry.'

'I trusted you,' he complained like a spoilt child.

'It's not your arm at all, it's your shoulder,' I told him. 'I can make a sling like you do for a broken collar bone. That should make it easier for you.'

'So long as you don't make me lie with it in that pool like you did Devon,' he said, clutching his arm to his chest in exactly the position I would need it.

I got to my feet. 'Don't tempt me.' I went to get a towel and the straps from my rucksack.

It was late afternoon. Amina, Naomi and Devon had gone to explore the tunnels and find the ravine we had told them about. Charlie tagged along. Jag was still curled up in his crevice. Daniel sat with his back propped up against one of the walls, moving from time to time to try to get more comfortable. I had dozed off. Partly because I was still exhausted from the night before, but also because it was only way I could forget the emptiness in my stomach, and the dull aching at the back of my head.

While I slept I dreamt of a table overflowing with food. There were roast chickens, sides of beef and ham, a whole spit roasted suckling pig, bowls of roast potatoes and fries, lasagne, plate meat and potato pies, Lancashire hot pot, pasties, mountains of cup cakes, bowls of trifle, strawberries and cream, coronation curry, dim sum. I don't even like dim sum. It was like a Sunday Carvery and Christmas at my Nan's all rolled into one.

When I woke my mouth was dry, my lips stuck together, and the hunger was worse than ever. I drained my water bottle dry, and ferreted desperately in my pockets for the remaining three Pontefract cakes. Without a moment's hesitation I put them all in my mouth and began to suck them slowly.

'Mewing like a hungry cat when it's dreaming.'

I looked over my shoulder, catching Daniel in the beam of my lamp. He grinned wearily.

'You were,' he said. 'It was quite sweet really. Shame I didn't have a video camera.'

I was too tired to think of a reply. He swung his left arm and something bright and shiny flew through the air towards me. It bounced once and came to rest against my boots. I reached down and picked it up. It was the whistle.

'You'd better take charge of that,' he said. 'I'm right handed.' Then he closed his eyes, and went to sleep.

'You were right. There's no way out.''

Devon flopped down beside me.

'How's your ankle?' I said.

'Much better. At least I can walk on it but I wouldn't want to have to run or climb with it. It's my gut that's getting to me. Like someone's grabbed it with their hands and squeezed it dry.'

'I know what you mean,' I said. 'You'd better drink some water.'

'If I drink anymore I'll be pissing for Britain,' he said.

'I thought you were West Indian?' said Naomi squatting down on my other side.

'Second generation British,' he said. 'I've got triple nationality. I can play cricket for Jamaica, football for Sierra Leone, and piss for Britain.'

Our laughter woke Daniel, and surprised the others. To anyone listening down the long and winding tunnels it must have sounded like the hysterical cries of demented souls.

Chapter 22
Jag's Story

By midday I had sounded the whistle on two separate occasions; once by the wall between us and the rising water, once at the entrance to the ravine. No one had replied. To make matters worse, if that was possible, the lamps belonging to Devon, Daniel, and Naomi had failed. Now we were left with mine and Amina's. Our hunger was making everyone irritable and bickering had broken out between Devon, Jag and Naomi.

Daniel was no longer up to keeping the peace. I decided it was time for another story. Amina had gone off with Charlie down the side tunnel we were using as a loo. While they were gone I broached the subject.

'There's only Jag and Charlie to go,' said Devon. 'It's got to be Jag.'

'Why me? Why not him?' Jag protested.

'Because it's obvious he's not up to it,' said Devon. 'Anyway I can tell you Charlie's story while he's out of the way.'

'That can't be right,' said Naomi. 'It's his story. Anyway how do you know what he's going to say.'

'Because we were in that domestic violence refuge at the same time, and his mother got talking to mine.

They poured their hearts out by all accounts. My mum told me the gist of it.'

'You should have told us,' said Naomi.

'I'm telling you now,' he replied.

'You'd better get on with it then,' she said. 'They'll be back in a minute.'

Devon shifted his position so that he had a clear view of the tunnel down which they both would come. 'According to my mum,' he began. 'Charlie's dad was a complete waste of space. He was hardly ever at home and when he was there he never had any time for Charlie. He got involved with a bad lot and ended up driving a getaway car on a raid on a supermarket in Didsbury. Only they didn't get away did they? Charlie's dad ended up in Strangeways on a six year stretch. In the meantime Charlie's mum had a string of men friends, and Charlie had one new "uncle" after another. All they cared was that he was out of the way. Never seen and never heard. The last one even went so far as to lock Charlie and his little brother Wayne in a cupboard under the stairs whenever he wanted to be alone with their mother. Sometimes they were in there all night.'

'No wonder he's terrified of the dark,' said Naomi.

'When Charlie's dad came out of prison he and this uncle set to. Charlie's dad came off worse and hasn't been seen since. Finally this uncle started drinking heavily and turned violent, towards the kids and Charlie's mum. That's why she was in the refuge hostel. The police got an injunction against the uncle, he beggared off to find another victim, and Charlie, Wayne, and his mum went back to their council house. Only she's the one with the drink problem now. Some days she's completely out of it. There's no food in the house and no one to do the washing. Apparently Charlie's the carer in that house. He makes the meals, such as they are, takes the clothes to the laundrette, collects his mother's prescriptions, gets Wayne up, washed and off to school every morning. That's why he's always late.'

'That's terrible,' said Naomi. 'Why does nobody help him?'

'Because nobody knows.'

'You know.'

'But I'm not supposed to. And anyway who am I going to tell?'

'Mr Taylor, our Head of Year,' I suggested.

'And what's he going to do?'

'You won't find out if you don't tell him,' said Naomi.

The beam from a lamp bounced off the angle of the tunnel wall and lit his face in profile. He moved his body back towards the centre of the circle.

'You never heard this from me,' he whispered.

'I don't feel so good,' Jag complained.

'Stop moaning.' said Devon. 'And get it over with. There's only you left.'

'What will we do when we've all told our stories?' Said Naomi.

'I don't know. Start again I suppose,' Devon responded. 'One thing at a time. Get on with it Jag. And don't think you can get away with any of that rubbish about your crew and all the fictional adventures you get up to. I know about gangs remember.'

Jag's Story

'What d'you want me to say?' Jag said. 'D'you wanna do it for me?'

'The rest of us Jag, have had the courage to tell our own stories,' said Amina kindly. 'To talk about things we have never shared with anyone else. It was not easy but speaking for myself I am glad that I did.'

'Me too,' said Naomi.

'And me.' Daniel and I chimed in together.

'That goes for me too,' said Devon.

Charlie squirmed beside him. Devon whispered something in his ear, and placed an arm around his shoulder.

Jag sat there silently.

Amina's torch was switched off. Mine sat in the middle of our circle. I had directed it towards the roof but someone must have accidentally touched it with their feet because it was now angled slightly towards the pool behind us. The refracted light cast shadows behind each of us, exaggerating both our shapes and sizes.

Jag took a deep breath, raised his head and pulled back his shoulders. His lengthening shadow climbed the wall.

'There's this stuff on the internet,' he began. 'You know, on Facebook and You Tube and stuff. About a sort of Hindu cult involving trannies.'

'Transvestites,' said Devon in response to Amina's puzzled expression. 'Men who dress up as women; like in the Gay Village.'

'And these ones do it so they can be closer to God,' Jag continued. 'They dress up like the Goddess Radha, so they can please Krishna her lover, the avatar of

Vishnu the Supreme Being. An' it's not just dressin' up; some of them live like women all the time.'

'That's because trannies are transgender,' said Naomi. 'Unlike transvestites who just dress like women.'

'There are loads of women cross dressers too,' said Devon. 'It's not just men. Anyway, what's this got to do with anything?'

'Give Jag break,' said Daniel. 'Let him tell it his way. Like the rest of us.' He paused between each phrase to catch his breath. It was obvious that he was in more pain than he had let on. I wondered if he might have injured his collarbone too.

'Thing is,' said Jag. 'My uncle DevJag, or Deepa as he now calls himself, is one of them. When my Dad found out he went off on one like a mad man. I mean like real crazy.'

'Not your problem,' Devon muttered.

'Yeh it is,' said Jag, pushing away a stone distractedly. 'Because now he's got it into his head that I'm gay.'

Devon's laugh was cut short by a sharp dig in the ribs from Naomi.

'One of my mates suddenly decided to call me Fag instead of Jag; like for a laugh.'

'Some mate,' said Daniel, breaking his own rule. Jag ploughed on.

'The others thought it was hilarious. Only it didn't stop there. Some idiots started sending texts about me to their mates. Even posted lies about me on their social networks. Someone tipped off one of my sisters. She told my mother. She had a nervous breakdown. My Dad went ballistic. I tried to tell him it's rubbish but he says the fact I hang around with boys all the time and I'm uncomfortable with girls even though I've got three sisters, proves it's true. The worst is he says even if I'm not gay the rumours still shame the family. He says he's gonna' arrange a marriage for me to chase away the gossip. He's already started looking for a suitable bride.'

'That's a bit drastic,' said Naomi.

'It can happen in Muslim families too,' said Amina. 'I know of men who are openly gay who are forced to marry and then bring their male partners to live with them and their wives.'

'It's not just Muslim and Hindu cultures,' I told her. 'I've heard it happens in some Christian communities too. Wherever there's homophobia.'

'And women and girls are treated like property to be sold off, end disputes between families, or sort out male problems,' said Naomi bitterly.

Thing is,' said Jag disconsolately. 'I haven't had sex with a girl. I haven't even kissed one. I'm beginning to wonder if I am...you know...gay."

'That doesn't mean a thing,' said Daniel. 'Loads of people haven't.'

'According to the poll in City Streets Magazine forty percent of 15 year olds have had sex,' said Devon,

Forty percent *say* they've had sex,' said Daniel. 'That doesn't mean they actually have.'

'OK,' Devon responded. Let's do our own poll. Who here has had sex?'

He raised his hand. His was the only one.

'Come on, don't be bashful, there's only us down here,' he said. 'Chatsworth House Rules remember.

'Chatham House.' Amina reminded him.

'Whatever,' he said.

'I've done girl on girl kissing,' said Naomi. 'Sort of experimenting. Does that count?'

'No way,' he said. 'What about you Charlie?'

Charlie, head down between his knees, had already retreated into his shell. Now he was rocking slowly back and forth.

'Leave him alone,' I said.

You're right,' said Devon. 'I shouldn't have picked on you Charlie. I'm sorry.' Charlie seemed not to have heard. Devon looked around at the rest of us. 'Nobody else? OK that's one out of six. What's that in percentages?'

'Sixteen percent,' said Amina.

'Come on guys, that's way below average.'

'Not in the States,' said Naomi. 'It's fifteen percent back home.'

'Whatever,' he said. 'So how come I'm the only one?'

'My religion forbids it,' said Amina. 'It would shame my father and me, and also my mother's memory. In any case I believe the act of love is far too precious to use it as a form of short term pleasure, or entertainment, like computer games or smoking, or drinking alcohol. It would demean it.'

'It isn't like that,' said Devon defensively. 'Not for me anyway. I've only ever done it with girls I really liked.'

'Liked, but not respected,' she replied. 'Or you would have considered the risk to their emotional and physical health. To their reputations, and perhaps to their future careers.'

'That's not fair,' he retorted. 'They could have said no.'

'That's easy to say,' Naomi joined in. 'When you care about someone, and you think everyone else is at it, that you're the only one that's missing out, and they keep asking if you've done it yet.'

'Especially when you've been on the alcopops,' said Daniel cupping his left hand under his elbow and lifting it slightly to relief the pressure on his shoulder.

'So who are you saving yourself for?' Devon asked him

'It's not that simple,' he said. 'Mostly, I agree with Amina. Plus I'd be terrified of getting a girl pregnant. That would complicate so much for both of us.'

'Have you never heard of contraception?' Devon chided.

''The day it's guaranteed one hundred percent safe I'll take the risk.'

'Then you'll die a virgin. What about you Grace?'

'I agree with Daniel,' I said. 'I think I'll know when the time is right.'

I still haven't met a boy I'd really trust with something so important to me. Not that there haven't been a few who wanted me to. But they were only interested in themselves; in impressing their friends, or chalking up another little victory. I'm never going to be reduced to someone else's bragging rights. There was one boy, Alan, who I really fancied, and who I know really fancied me. Then he went and let Karina take him for a ride. I never dreamt that he was that weak, that shallow, so easily swayed. After that experience he came on to me, but it was too late. Karina's nickname is the school bicycle; everyone gets to ride her at least once. That's so gross isn't it? Imagine carrying that label around for the rest of your life. Not me. I'm going to keep saying no until I'm ready. How hard can that be?

'Good luck Jag,' said Devon sounding like he meant it. 'If nothing else, they've proved you're normal. That should help.'

Jag shook his head disconsolately. 'Try telling my father,' he said. 'I think I'm gonna have to get laid just to get him off my case.' He looked towards me. 'Can we stop this now Grace?' he appealed. 'I don't feel good.'

I don't know why he asked me. Perhaps it was because I was holding the whistle.

'Of course we can,' I said.

Devon got up, went over to Jag, and offered him his water bottle.

'Well done,' he said. 'And you know something else *bruv*? You never said *innit*; not even once.'

Chapter 23

It was four o'clock in the afternoon. Fifty miles to the South our classmates would be arriving home from school. Singletons, in their offices, would be deciding which ready meal-for-one to pickup up from the supermarket Express on the corner. The first wave of the evening rush hour would be winding its way out of the city desperate to miss the bumper-to-bumper jams all the way down Deansgate and out onto Chapel Street, Rochdale Road, and Princess Parkway.

Not one of us had anything left to eat. What little conversation followed Jag's story had long since petered out. Daniel, Jag and Charlie appeared to be asleep. My headache had returned and together with the hunger and the change in temperature I found it impossible to join them. Our new home was damper and cooler than either of our previous ones; some kind of cold trap. There was a movement to my left. It was Naomi. In the fading light from my near exhausted lamp I realised that she was shivering uncontrollably. She caught my gaze.

'This sodding cold!' she complained.

'Why don't we light a fire,' said Devon.

'What with?' I asked.

'The wooden rungs from that rope ladder. We can

use the food wrappers to get it started,' he said. 'It's a good job Daniel made us pick them up.'

'It'll mean waking the others up,' I said.

'Then do it. Better than letting them freeze to death.'

I thought that was something of an exaggeration, but he wasn't far out.

We sat in a small circle, very nearly close enough to touch each other, embracing the heat, listening to the spit and crackle of the wood as the fire engulfed it, transfixed by the orange and yellow flames flickering before us. There was something primitive, primeval, about the scene. I could imagine our ancestors sitting in caves like this tens of thousands of years ago, perhaps in this one even, tearing at the flesh of butchered animals like deer and wild cats. I wondered if they had ever practiced cannibalism in periods of famine or when the ice and snow cut them off for weeks at a time.

Without intending to I found myself remembering the film *Alive* about the Uruguayan rugby team and their families stranded in the Andes following a plane crash. Sixteen of the forty five had survived but only by eating the flesh of their dead companions. Would any of us here, I wondered, find ourselves resorting to such a practice. My grim and melancholy thoughts were rudely interrupted.

'Get it off you pillock!'

Devon was on his feet wafting smoke from in front of his face. Daniel pulled with his feet at a smoking piece of rope he had presumably thrown onto the fire. As he stamped on the smouldering cord the rest of us moved back out of range of the black acrid smoke.

'I'm sorry...' he started to say.

Jag cut him off. 'Where's that smoke goin'?' he said.

'What do you mean?' asked Naomi.

'Look,' he said, pointing.

Amina switched on her lamp and followed the swirling mass of smoke as it crept along the roof across the pool, and into the tunnel beyond it.

'He's right,' said Naomi. 'It should just hang around in here. There must a draught somewhere that's sucking it out.'

'That doesn't mean it's a way out does it?' said Devon. 'It could be a hole the size of a golf ball.'

'It's worth a look though, surely?' I said.

'Anything's gotta be better than sittin' waitin' to die,' said Jag.

It was the first time anyone had mentioned that word, even though it must have been on all of our minds from day one. Hearing it out loud like that was like we'd all been given an electric shock.

''Why don't you and Amina go and have a look?' said Daniel.

'I'm comin' too,' said Jag.

'I'm might as well too,' said Devon.

In the end, we all went. Nobody wanted to be left behind. Before we left Daniel kicked the rope back onto the fire, and added the other piece. He figured that we would need as much smoke as possible if we were going to be able to follow it. He was right.

'Where the hell's it gone?' said Devon.

The six of us stood squeezed into the space where the narrow ravine ended. Water ran down the walls and dripped continuously on our heads. My lamp had failed completely but Amina was busy scanning the walls with hers, desperately seeking the slightest wisp of smoke. The beam picked out clumps of green and brown algae clinging stubbornly to the rock. That means there must be some natural light up there I told myself.

'There!' shouted Daniel. No...back a bit... back ... back...stop!'

It was barely perceptible, until she managed to hold the lamp still with both her hands. A grey black curl of smoke wound its way up the sheer limestone before disappearing beyond the natural bridge that spanned the gap between the walls some twenty metres above our heads.

'If there is a hole I can't see it being big enough for us to get through,' said Devon. 'In any case, how are we going to get up there to find out?'

That cold hand clutched at my heart again stilling the excitement that had been gathering there. He was right. Devon's ankle was much improved but it wouldn't support him climbing that rock face. Daniel, the obvious choice, was out of action. Jag was clearly no longer up to it, Naomi would never have the strength, and Charlie was far too timid. That left Amina and me.

'I'll go,' I said.

The boys protested but they knew that it was the only solution; Amina or me. Amina was willing to try but she was the least experienced climber of us all. In the end, it was agreed. I would give it my best.

I placed the loop of Matt's rope over my head, under my arms, and across my body. The idea was that if I made it to the top I would secure it at the top to aid my descent, and in case there was any point in the others using it to join me up there. The ascenders and descenders were attached to my belt. Amina's lamp was now on my helmet. I stood at the foot of the rock fall, and found my first hand hold. It was too late to turn back now.

Slowly but steadily I climbed. Within touching distance of the slab of rock that formed the bridge between the walls I paused to catch my breath, and ease the tension in my hands and legs. I clenched and unclenched the fingers of each hand in turn. My fingernails were all but gone, and my hands badly scratched. The pain in the muscles of my thighs and calves was excruciating, as though a fire raged through them. It was not the height I had climbed, but the steepness of the ascent that had been so punishing.

'Are you alright Grace?' shouted Daniel out of the darkness below.

'I'm just about to get onto the bridge,' I told him. 'Those of you who believe in God, you'd better start praying that it's going to hold me.'

The thought had not occurred to me until then. Now I was scared stiff. It took every ounce of courage to move my left foot up to a higher point so that I could lever my body onto the bridge. Courage didn't come into it. I had little option. To try to go back down without the lamp to help me, and without the rope secured, would have been suicidal.

I held my breath as I lowered my chest onto the slab of limestone and let it take the weight of my body. So far so good.

'I'm there,' I told them.

'Can you see where the smoke's going? Is there an

opening of some kind...a fissure? ' It was Devon's voice I think.

'Not yet,' I replied. 'I'm going to tie on the rope first, then I'll have a look. It may take some time.'

It was a good ten minutes because I had to loop the rope around the rock as close as I dare to the rock face, and tie it off, then attach the descenders. It was only then that it occurred to me that I should have left the ascenders at the bottom for the next person to use.

'I'm sorry,' I told them. 'I should have left the ascenders down there with you.' I heard a muted curse. 'If you let me know when you've backed up I'll drop them down to you,' I said.

'Give us a minute,' said Daniel.

I could hear them shuffling backwards into the narrowest part of the ravine.

'OK!' shouted Devon.

I let them go and heard the clatter as they bounced off the rock face and landed on the floor of the ravine.

'Got them!' shouted Devon a moment later.

Now I felt able to look around. Three metres above my head was a ceiling of solid rock. A similar distance to my left was the end wall of the ravine; behind me, the rock pile I had climbed. Straight ahead however, where the bridge became part of the furthest wall, was a squeeze about a foot in height and perhaps a foot and a half in width. With luck this would be where the smoke was heading. I wrapped my arms and legs around the edges of the bridge and eased myself towards it inches at a time. The closer I got the wetter, more slippery, and more treacherous it became. With a foot to go I felt a cool draught on my face. My heart began to beat faster with anticipation, and I felt the veins throbbing in my neck. I loosened the strap around my chin a notch, and gingerly edged forward.

'What's happening?' Someone shouted.

''I've found a small passage – a squeeze,' I said. 'Give me a minute, it's really slippery up here.'

'Take your time Grace.' This time it was Daniel. I could hear the pain in his voice. 'Just be careful.'

'I will.'

The squeeze went into the rock for about two metres at which point it widened slightly, and then finished at a limestone face. I closed my eyes, switched off my lamp, and waited for my eyes to accustom themselves to the darkness. When I opened them again, there it was, exactly as I expected. A small shaft of light slanted down from somewhere above. It could only mean one thing. There was an opening to the surface.

It lit only the area immediately below the source. I tried to estimate the circumference of that light. Then I realised that the only thing that really mattered was its diameter. It was something close to two thirds of a metre; equivalent to the widest part of the squeeze. This was no cleft or fissure. Probably it had started as a fissure but surface run off had widened it into a sink hole flowing down into the ravine.

My initial enthusiasm waned with the realisation that none of us – with the possible exception of Charlie, or maybe Naomi who was far too weak – would be able to crawl into the squeeze and contort our bodies in such a way as to be able to climb up into that passage. Even then there was no guarantee that it was climbable, or that it didn't narrow before reaching the surface.

'What's going on Grace?' Devon shouted.
I told them.

'That's it then,' said Daniel. 'There's no other option. Charlie, you're going to have to do it.'

Every other minute, for twenty minutes, I had been sounding the distress calls without success. The only option left was to try the mobile phones again. There was no signal down in the ravine but Naomi had pointed out that there was more chance closer to the surface and without the obstacle provided by the limestone walls. The idea was for Charlie to climb the rock pile, crawl into the squeeze, stand up in the vertical passage, and make a call. It sounded great, in theory.

In the failing light from Amina's lamp I could just make out Charlie's heart-rending silhouette. Tiny, malnourished, slump shouldered, he stood head bowed, as sad and lonely as I had ever seen him. Remembering the pithy story Devon had shared with us about him only made it worse.

'You'll be alright Charlie,' I called down. 'I'll be right here with you all the way.'

Except for the climb up of course.

'There you go,' said Devon. 'A piece of cake. You'll be attached to the rope all the way up, and Grace will be waiting at the top.'

'Your chance to be a hero,' I heard Jag say.

Amina placed her arm around Charlie's shoulders and led him off a few paces away from the others, which was as much as she could manage in that confined space. It was impossible to hear what she was saying but after less than a minute she guided him back to the foot of the rock pile.

'Charlie is ready,' she said.

Seizing the moment Devon began to attach the first of the ascenders to Charlie's harness. Amina held out her hand. 'You'd better give me both of your phones,' she said. 'In case one doesn't work or is dropped.'

Naomi handed over hers. 'I've switched it on,' she said. 'To make it easier for him.'

I could see the green glow of the screen.

'Here's mine,' said Devon.

I watched as they put them in the jackets of Charlie's pockets and zipped them closed.

'Off you go then,' said Devon. The words sounded brutally casual but the manner in which he said them was supportive, compassionate even.

Charlie grasped the rope with one hand, placed his left foot on the rock pile, and leant forward. For a moment I thought he had frozen, but he pulled himself up, slid the ascender up the rope, and found his next secure footing. It was nothing short of a miracle. Several times his foot slipped and losing his hold on the rope he hung there, dangling like the proverbial puppet on a string. But each time he recovered and started up again. In less than five minutes I was hauling him up onto the bridge beside me.

'Charlie, that was amazing,' I said. 'No, hold that, *you* were amazing.'

The pupils of his eyes widened with pleasure until my beam caught his face full on, forcing him to shield them with his hand. He almost slipped and I had to grab him and pull him towards me.

'Are you two alright?' Daniel called anxiously.

'We're fine,' I said. Hoping that was true.

Chapter 24

Charlie took off his over jacket and trousers. He squeezed himself into the narrow passage and crawled the short distance to the end. He rolled over onto his back and levered himself up into a seating position, his back against the wall.

'Well done, Charlie,' I said. 'Can you see anything?'

He looked up into the space above him, and squinted.

'It's like a pipe,' he said. 'With some light at the end.'

'Daylight?'

'I think so.'

'Can you see anything else?'

'There's some stuff hanging down from the top. And something sort of green and feathery covering part of the opening.'

I racked my brain, trying to make sense of the image. ''Could it be a fern?'

'Yeh, it must be.'

'How far away is it?'

'I dunno. About three times my height I suppose.'

Fifteen feet. Just under five metres.

'Do you think you could climb up there?'

His response was immediate. He shook his head.

'There's no chance Grace. I'm sorry but there's nothing to hang onto. It's smooth...like glass, and wet and slippery.'

'OK,' I said. 'No need to be sorry. It's not your fault. You're doing just fine. It's time to make that call Charlie. Try Naomi's phone first.'

He took it from his trouser pocket.

'Have you got a signal?' I said.

'I don't think so.'

Try it anyway.

'Who shall I call?' he said.

'What's he saying?' Devon shouted.

'He wants to know who to call.'

'Tell him 911' Naomi shouted.

'It's 999 over here,' Devon reminded her

'Or 112,' said Daniel.

'You're only confusing him,' I told them. 'Listen Charlie, it's 999.'

I waited for him to dial.

'It's no good,' he said. 'There's nothing.'

I could feel hope draining away.

'Try Devon's,' I said.

He placed Naomi's phone on the floor beside him and tugged Devon's phone from his other pocket. I saw the screen light up.

'I think I've got a signal,' he said excitedly. 'But there's only one bar.'

'Try standing up,' I said.

He anchored his little feet on the floor of the passage and shuffled his bottom up the wall behind him until all I could see were his skinny legs from the knees down.

'Try it now,' I said.

It must only have been twenty seconds or so, but it seemed like an age.

'I've got through Grace!' He shouted. 'I'm through!'

Calm down Charlie,' I told him. 'Just answer their questions.'

I heard them cheering down below. I thought it far too premature.

'They want to know where we are.'

'What did he say?' shouted Devon.

'They want to know where we are.'

'Tell them to triangulate on the phone,' yelled Jag. 'They're quick enough to do it when they wanna find a drug dealer.'

'Charlie, Tell them we're about 600 metres North East from where the tunnel collapsed, and about 15 metres below the hillside,' I suggested.

I could have been way out, but all along I had been using my compass, and trying to estimate how far we'd travelled each time we moved camp.

'And tell them I'll sound our distress call with the whistle for one minute every five minutes until they get here.'

Shortly afterwards Charlie slid down the wall and his face appeared in the centre of my beam. He was grinning from ear to ear.

I blew that whistle on five separate occasions before Charlie and I finally heard the chopping sound of a helicopter hovering above us, followed two minutes later by a man's anxious voice.

'Hello...Charlie...are you there?'

I can't describe how it felt. I know that tears trickled down my cheeks with relief and jubilation one minute, and with sorrow for those we would be leaving behind the next.

They quickly determined that the sink hole would have to be made wider, and that we would just have to be patient. All except for Charlie. He was thin enough for them to be able to lower a rope with a harness and pull him out. As they started to haul him up I told the others. They cheered and hooted and clapped their hands. Above it all I heard Daniel's voice.

'Bravo Charlie,' he shouted. 'Onwards and upwards!'

The next sixteen hours were a massive anti-climax. Although they'd managed to pull Charlie out it was evident that neither we nor any members of the rescue team were going to be able to negotiate that chimney as it currently was, let alone the passage that led to it.

They lowered down in baskets thermal blankets, vacuum flasks of hot soup, some bread rolls, and bottles of water, which I then lowered to the others in the ravine. I didn't fancy climbing down to join them, even with the assistance of the rope. This close to safety I wasn't taking any chances. I spent the night perched on the bridge, my back against the furthest wall, listening to the sounds of the drill, and the water they were using for lubrication as it cascaded out of the squeeze and down into the ravine.

It was seventeen minutes past eleven on the morning of the Friday the third of June when I found myself hauled clear of the mouth of the bore hole, and gently lowered onto the heather. We had only been trapped underground for four days and nights. I know it doesn't sound long but when the Grim Reaper has already visited, you have no contact with the outside world, no likelihood of rescue anytime soon, and your food has run out, it feels like forever.

Everything on the hillside seemed so fresh and stark. I drank in the clear blue sky, the warmth of the sun, the yellow and white carpet of rock-rose, bird's-foot trefoil, and limestone bedstraw, and the smell of wild thyme crushed beneath our boots. The warmth of my mother's arms as she hugged me to her chest. The tears on my father's cheeks.

Chapter 25

It took four months for them to recover the bodies. Our assumption had been correct. That minor earthquake had led a section of the tunnel to collapse, diverting one of the underground streams that fed Leck Beck. Not only that, but it had drained an entire lake into the cavern where we had first laid up, which is what had forced us to move on. The pressure of water had finally burst through the rock fall that had cut us off carrying the bodies of Miss Walsh, Matt, and Wesley into the cavern. It was from there that they were finally recovered.

Matt's funeral was in Bicester, his home town, on the same day that Miss Walsh and Wesley were laid to rest. I went to both of those funerals, along with all of Years 10 and 11. Mum and Dad said I didn't have to, but I'm glad I did. It was a chance to say goodbye, and to reflect on how lucky I had been. Seeing the faces of their grieving families, knowing that they would be asking the question why it had happened to them, I had a question of my own. Why had I been one of the lucky ones? Was it chance, or destiny? Was there something I was supposed to do with my life that could possibly justify their loss, and my good fortune? I am still waiting for the answer.

Naomi and Jag both had to stay in hospital for a few days while they were given a renourishment programme. A gradual introduction of food with a balance of fluids and the correct minerals and electrolytes. I didn't really understand it but Rhianna is doing biochemistry and she explained it to me. She said that a lot of the victims of concentration camps – like Belsen and Theresienstadt where Daniels relatives had perished - died after they were rescued because they were fed too much food too quickly and their bodies couldn't process it properly, draining what little resources their bodies had just to cope with the digestion process. How sad is that?

The rest of us it seems had been living on our fat supplies, like camels. I'll never complain again about being size twelve.

Devon left school at the end of Year 10 but he goes to college for evening and day release courses. He started with a major supermarket chain, and they were so impressed that after only a year and a half they've told him he can join their trainee store management scheme. He could be on £50,000 by the time he's twenty five years old. Who said there are no opportunities for young people these days?

Naomi has gone back to the States. She's in her freshman year aiming for a BA in Philosophy. I've no idea what she's going to do with that but she says her experience under the Pennines with us was worth a whole year's credits. Something about the Greek Philosopher Plato's *Allegory of the Cave*. We still keep in touch by email and Skype from time to time, and we're friends on Facebook. We don't talk about it, but from the photo's she posts it looks like she's gone up a size in weight, and held it there. She still looks fragile but she's happy and that's much more important isn't it?

Amina's father is still with Médecins Sans Frontières, but he lives in France and because of his work and refugee status he has been granted French citizenship. As a result, it seems Amina is no longer at risk of deportation, or having to undergo an arranged marriage just to stay here, which is brilliant. She has offers to study Medicine at Manchester, London and Newcastle Universities, and if her mocks are anything to go by she'll sail through.

Daniel is studying A Level English with me, Economics, French and General Studies. Oh yes, and Mandarin Chinese on the side. He's applied to read PPE at Oxford – that's Philosophy, Politics and Economics. He talks of going into politics. I think he's perfectly suited. He has the charisma, and there was all that stuff he said about the maintenance of hope. I wouldn't be surprised if he was Prime Minister one day. He'd get my vote. Before I wrote this part I did ask him where he got the idea of establishing a routine. It was from what he remembered reading about the trapped Chilean miners.

'Routine helped to keep them sane,' he said. 'Us too.'

It just goes to prove the power of reading. You never know when something you've read might just save your life.

Jag is at College on some kind of IT course. I saw him in town last Saturday. He was with his mates, and pretended not to see me but Asif, the leader of his crew, called me over. I went for Jag's sake, so he wouldn't lose face.

'Hey Grace,' said Asif. 'Have you heard the one about the archaeologists and the cave'

'No,' I said. 'I'm not sure I want to.'

'Oh you'll love this, girl,' said one of his acolytes bouncing up and down in a poor imitation of Spellbound. 'Tell her Jag.'

Jag squirmed, and shook his head. I could have sworn he was blushing. 'I forget the endin' innit,' he said.

Asif gave him a withering look, and turned to me. 'Two archaeologists in a cave in Israel,' he began. 'They find these pictures on the wall. There's a dog, a donkey, a shovel, a fish an' a star of David. They date these pictures to three thousand five hundred years BC. They ain't seen nothing like it before. Can't decide if it's art, a story, or some kind of message. They take their finding to a professor an' a rabbi. The professor, he says: 'It's simple man. These people domesticated the wild dog as a guard an' a companion. The donkey carried their heavy stuff. They invented the shovel and used it to farm. The fish shows they were fishermen too. The Star of David tells us these intelligent people were Israelites.' The rabbi shakes his head. 'Don't you know that Hebrew is written from right to left?' he says. 'This is early Hebrew graffiti. It reads: Holy mackerel; dig the ass on that bitch!' '

At which they all collapsed with laughter. All except Jag, who looked sheepish and shrugged his shoulders by way of apology. I thought that was encouraging; a start.

Devon told me that all those evil emails and rumours about Jag had stopped. He claimed it was down to Jag's relative hero status from surviving the cave, not to mention the way he'd big- upped his part in it. From what I heard the real reason is that Devon had put the word round that his brother Jerome and his crew would sort out anyone who continued to spread those lies. Devon may not be part of the gang culture but he's obviously not averse to using his connections to do some good. As for Jag's relationship with his dad it turns out Jag did exactly what he threatened to do, and got himself laid. Poor Karina again I'm afraid. Whether that means he's resolved his gender orientation or not only time will tell.

As for Charlie, when the police went round to his house to tell his mother he was missing they found Wayne sitting in a mess, watching the television, and his mother comatose on the kitchen floor. They called in Social Services. Charlie and his brother went into foster care while their mother went into rehab. They're back with her now and although she still binge drinks from time to time Charlie told Amina it's nowhere near as bad. The council provided a cleaner once a week, and a health visitor and a social worker call regularly to make sure they're alright.

He seems to have grown up overnight. I think it's because he knows he no longer has to cope all on his own. He's got a new tag too; *CBO* aka Charlie Bravo Echo. Devon gave it him because of what Daniel shouted in the cave: *"Bravo Charlie!"* And the echo that followed it. I think that's neat. I swear he looks inches taller whenever people call him it in public. He's at the same supermarket as Devon; not on the management course but stacking shelves and checking deliveries. Still, you never know. At least he's a got a mentor there to encourage him, and maybe even give him a leg up.

I applied to read English at London University, Warwick, York, Exeter, and the BA in English Literature with Creative Writing at East Anglia Uni. I'm holding an offer from London as my preference, and East Anglia as my insurance. Now all I've got to do is get the grades.

I need to get away. Things are better now between me and my parents but there are too many memories here. I hate the idea of leaving university with such a large debt around my neck but I know I don't have to start paying it back until I can afford to, and everyone else will be in the same boat. Some things are worth paying for.

I'm going to take a Gap Year if they'll let me. Mainly so I can earn some money to keep that debt down. I've been working in a hotel at weekends for the past year and they say they'll take me on full time; hardly surprising on those wages. Looking on the bright side, it'll give me a chance to brush up on my Polish and Czech – and in case you haven't worked that out you should know that I'm laughing out loud.

My pastoral tutor said I should apply to Cambridge or Oxford. I know that mum and dad would have liked me to, but I wasn't convinced. Daniel said all the other Universities would be asking for A* grades so I'd nothing to lose by applying. He said the Personal Statement would make all the difference and there are not many people who've had an experience like ours to draw on.

I was going back over my personal statement the other day, trying to figure out exactly what it is I've learned from those four days underground. Well, firstly, nothing is ever as it seems. As for people, and

I include myself in this, there is so much more to them than you would ever guess. More often than not what you can see is nothing compared to what's going on below the surface, just like swans swimming.

It's also like our shadows on the cave walls. Every one of them one was unique, and instantly recognisable. But if that shadow was all you had to go on you'd know nothing about us whatsoever. If you want to understand someone you have to listen. Really listen.

I've also discovered that some people can't bear silence. They have to fill it. Other people need silence. It's where they do their thinking, and their healing.

I've done a lot of thinking since we came out, and a lot of reading too. One of the papers – probably the Guardian because we have to read it for General Studies - compared our experience with that of a group of boys stranded on an deserted tropical island in *The Lord of The Flies*; a novel by William Golding. I found a copy in the school library. They started by electing a leader called Ralph. We didn't choose anyone, Daniel simply emerged, and we were happy to let him lead. But I think all of us were leaders in one way or another. On the island it was very different. It wasn't long before Ralph's leadership was challenged and the group split into two camps. Fuelled by fear, their hostility towards each other quickly led to bloodshed and killing as the beast inside each of them fought its way to the surface.

I wasn't the least bit surprised. If you let men run anything on their own they'll make a mess of it: government; the banks; religion; especially religion. Take Judaism, Christianity, and Islam; three great religions with the same founding history, and the same God. They've been at each other's throats in one way or another for centuries. Not only that, each of them has split into factions at war with each other, just like the boys on that desert island. As far as I can see they've lost their way. They may have started off trying to make meaning of the world, the universe, and our place within it, but pretty soon it became less about belief, and more about behaviour, ownership, and control. They need to reconnect with young people, and embrace women, not just as mothers and homemakers but as equals.

I haven't lost my faith, though. If anything it's got stronger. I think I need for there to be a heaven, otherwise what's it all for? And where are Wesley, Matt, and poor Miss Walsh right now? But one thing I've learned for sure; God doesn't interfere. I don't believe he chose who was going to die in that cave, and who would survive. Otherwise what's the point of having free will if your fate has already been decided? When it comes down to it, you've got your life, whatever talents you were born with, and the Earth beneath your feet. After that it's up to you what you make of it. But you don't have to do it alone.

I've come to terms with all the kindness people at our church insist on directing my way. Maybe it's because I don't feel guilty any more. And to be honest that sense of community is the main reason I still attend.

My Dad – you'll already have noticed that I don't call him father anymore - told me about a play called *No Exit* by Jean Paul Sartre, a French writer. It's about a man and two women, in the afterlife, locked up in a room for all eternity as a punishment for the lives they led.   He said the theme of the play is that hell is other people, but only if we allow their judgements of us to affect the way we see ourselves.   I've learned that it doesn't have to be like that.   Heaven can be other people too.   It's just a question of how you treat them.

Yesterday I persuaded Dad to drive me back to the moors.   Amina asked if she could come too.   When we arrived to pick her up Charlie was waiting with her.

The three of us climbed the track down which the rescuers had brought us, and across the limestone pavement towards the tops.   On the lower slopes we picked our way through swathes of purple moor grass and heath rush interspersed with patches of red and green moss.   Towards the summit the yellow and white of early summer had been replaced by tiny blue harebells nodding in the breeze.   Charlie pointed out a vivid sky-blue butterfly basking in the sun on the flower head of a field scabious.

In all the time we had been trapped beneath this place, not once had I thought of the beauty, serenity, and wildness of the hillside above us.   I'd missed my Mum and Dad, and my best friend Rachel. Not being able to text her, to post on her Facebook page, and have her posts on mine.   I missed Skins, and Glee, Holly Oaks and Coronation Street, and Justin Bieber, but apart from staying sane, and how we were going to get out of there, the only things my mind had really dwelt on were the people I would leave behind, how they would miss me; and the life and opportunities that I might never experience.

It struck me that that none of us - apart from Charlie who had better reason than any, and Jag in his moment of madness - had really cried full on until we came out of that place. And then we all did, but not for long. The funerals were the worst. That's when what Daniel said about survivors' guilt came home to me. But in reality we'd already faced up to that demon before any of us got out of the cave.

They insisted that we have counselling but after the first couple of sessions they decided that none of us needed it. We had counselled each other during our time in the cave, by listening to each other's stories. By helping each other to see those stories, and the beliefs, fears and hopes they represented, through someone else's eyes. By helping each other to reframe them, refine them, come to terms with them, and to move on.

Mrs Frank, our English teacher, says that everyone has a book in them. That we all have a story to tell. What I think I've discovered is that the way in which we tell that story to ourselves and others, and how we make sense of it, defines who we think we are. The kind of person we will become. We can stay trapped by the past, and even by the present, we can choose to see ourselves as victims, or we can set ourselves free to become the person we would like to be. From now on I'm going to surround myself with people who will listen to my story, help me to become that person, and are happy for me to do the same for them. That's how friendship should be.

The most important thing I learned in that cave is that you only have one life, and the sooner you start living it the better. Sometimes it's really scary, just as Devon and Naomi said, but I've learned that there's nothing that can't be overcome.

I'm not sure what I'm going to do with the rest of my life. Right now I'm torn between social work and journalism. I'm talking serious journalism; the kind that exposes injustice, and helps people to make informed choices, not the kind that invades vulnerable people's privacy through illegal phone hacking just to satisfy unhealthy curiosity.

Whatever I end up doing I just hope, in some small way, to make the world a better place to live in for my children, and their children. And to be true to myself.

As ever, Daniel was right.

Onward and upward!

On Sunday 6 November 2011, just as The Cave was being published, The Misty Mountain Mud Miners broke through the last few feet of mud and rock to join up 64 miles of tunnels and caves linking Cumbria, Lancashire, and Yorkshire, to create the longest continuous cave system in Great Britain, and accomplish a 50 year old dream. This eBook version is also dedicated to them, and to their amazing achievement.

When we dream about how the future might be we are setting goals for ourselves, but only if we then strive to make them a reality.

The Author

Formerly Principal Inspector of Schools for the City of Manchester, Head of the Manchester School Improvement Service, and Lead Network Facilitator for the National College of School Leadership, Bill has numerous publications to his name in the field of education. For four years he was also a programme consultant and panellist on the popular live Granada Television programme *Which Way*, presented by the iconic, and much missed, Tony Wilson. He has written six crime thriller novels to date – all of them based in and around the City of Manchester.

His first novel *The Cleansing* was short listed for the Long Barn Books Debut Novel Award.
Bill was awarded the ePublishing Consortium Writers Award 2011 for The Cleansing.

A Trace of Blood, in manuscript, reached the semi-final of the Amazon Breakthrough Novel Award.

If you've enjoyed
A Trace Of Blood
Try the other novels in the series:
The Cleansing
The Head Case
The Tiger's Cave
A Fatal Intervention
Bluebell Hollow
Available through Booksellers and Amazon as paperbacks and Kindle EBooks

www.billrogers.co.uk www.catonbooks.com

THE CLEANSING
ISBN: 978 1 906645 61 8
Grosvenor House Publishing

The novel that first introduced DCI Tom Caton.
Christmas approaches. A killer dressed as a clown haunts
the streets of Manchester. For him the City's miraculous
regeneration had unacceptable
consequences. This is the reckoning. DCI Tom Caton
enlists the help of forensic profiler Kate Webb,
placing her in mortal danger. The trail leads from the site
of the old mass cholera graves, through Moss
Side, the Gay Village, the penthouse opulence of
canalside apartment blocks, and the bustling
Christmas Market, to the Victorian Gothic grandeur of the
Town Hall. Time is running out: For Tom, for Kate...and
for the City.

Short listed for the
Long Barn Books Debut Novel Award

Bill was awarded the ePublishing Consortium Writers
Award 2011 for The Cleansing.

THE HEAD CASE
ISBN: 978 1 9564220 0 2

Roger Standing CBE, Head of Harmony High
Academy, and the Prime Minister's Special Adviser for
Education, is dead. DCI Tom Caton is not short of
suspects. But if this is a simple mugging, then why is MI5
ransacking Standing's apartment, and disrupting the
investigation? And why are the widow and her son taking
the news so calmly?

SOMETHING IS ROTTEN IN THE CORRIDORS
OF POWER.

THE TIGER'S CAVE
ISBN: 978 0 9564220 1 9

A lorry full of Chinese illegal immigrants arrives in Hull.
Twenty four hours later their bodies are discovered close
to the M62 motorway; but a young man and a girl are
missing, and still at risk.
Supported by the Serious and Organised Crime
Agency, Caton must travel to China to pick up the trail.
But he knows the solution is closer to home – in
Manchester's Chinatown - and time is running out.

A FATAL INTERVENTION
ISBN: 978-0-9564220-3-3

A SUCCESSFUL BARRISTER
A WRONGFUL ACCUSATION
A MYSTERIOUS DISAPPEARANCE

It's the last thing Rob Thornton expects. When he finds
his life turned upside down he sets out on the trail of
Anjelita Covas, his accuser. Haunted by her tragic history
and sudden disappearance Rob turns detective in
London's underworld. A series of rhyming messages
arrive, each signalling a murder. Rob must find Anjelita
and face a dark truth.

DEEP BENEATH THE CITY OF MANCHESTER LIES
A HEART OF DARKNESS

BLUEBELL HOLLOW
ISBN: 978 0 9564220-2-6

DCI Tom Caton's world is rocked when he learns that he has a son by a former lover. Then the first of the bodies is discovered at the Cutacre Open Cast Mine. The victims appear to have addiction in common. Suspects include a Premiership footballer, a barrister, and just about everyone at the Oasis Rehab Clinic in leafy Cheshire. As Caton digs deeper his world begins to fall apart.

A TRACE OF BLOOD
Paperback ISBN: 978-0-9564220-4-0

It is Fall in Manchester, New Hampshire. Niamh Caton buries her Aunt Miriam; victim of a senseless hit and run. Now she is alone in the world.

Three thousand miles away across the Big Pond, Detective Chief Inspector Tom Caton – on the verge of moving into a new apartment with his fiancée Kate, a Home Office profiler at the University - is surprised to learn that he and Niamh are cousins. He is drawn into her obsession to trace their ancestors, and search out any living relatives.

One by one new members of the Caton clan are unearthed - in County Kerry, where the Caton dynasty began; in Vermont; and in Manchester - and just as speedily dispatched. Niamh and Tom find themselves in a race against time, to find the perpetrator, before they become the killer's final victim and, quite literally, the end of the line.